GRINDING FROST

STARCROSSED DRAGONS BOOK 2

ERIN BEDFORD

J. A. CIPRIANO

WANT TO GET FREE STUFF?

<u>Sign up here.</u> If you do, I'll send you some free short stories.

Visit Erin on Facebook or on the web at ErinBedford.com.

The Underground

Chasing Rabbits

Chasing Cats

Chasing Princes

Chasing Shadows

Chasing Hearts

Fairy Tale Bad Boys

Hunter

Pirate

Thief

Mirror

Stepbrother

The Celestial War Chronicles

Song of Blood and Fire

Visions of War and Water

The Mary Wiles Chronicles

Marked By Hell

Bound By Hell

Deceived By Hell

Tempted By Hell

The Crimson Fold

Until Midnight

Vampire CEO

Granting Her Wish

ALSO BY J.A. CIPRIANO

<u>Starcrossed Dragons</u>

Riding Lightning

Grinding Frost

Swallowing Fire

Pounding Earth

<u>The Goddess Harem</u>

The Tiger's Offer

The Wolf's Hunt

The Dragon's War

<u>Justice Squad</u>

Miracle's Touch

<u>Her Angels</u>

Heaven's Embrace

Heaven's A Beach

Heaven's Most Wanted

The Shaman Queen's Harem

Ghosts and Grudges

1

Nothing was more awkward than having lunch with my family. Correction. Nothing was more awkward than having lunch with my family *and* all three of my current lovers. Even more so when one of them wouldn't stop pawing me under the table.

I flushed with pleasure and pushed at Firestar's hand for the third time, but he was relentless. His fingers dipped between my thighs, and I snapped my legs together to squeeze them out. I shot Firestar a warning look as I picked up my glass.

"So, Firestar," my sister, Aeis, started and looked up from her meal, eyes full of suspicion. "What exactly happened when Aeis came to see your father? I thought you and he weren't speaking?"

"We weren't," Firestar answered placing his hand on top of mine and smiling. "But Maya helped us work through our issues and come up with a plausible solution."

I gave Firestar a small smile in return not because it was expected, but because I genuinely liked seeing him. If it hadn't been for Firestar, I wouldn't be in the mess I was in now, but I didn't blame him for it. I'd known how my father would react when I'd brought Firestar home with me.

That wasn't the real problem though. Not really anyway. My anger had gotten the better of me, and I'd made a bad situation even worse.

When I'd announced I was pregnant, my father, while angry for a time, rejoiced at finally having an heir to our legacy.

My sister and mother had not.

They had both looked at me with suspicious eyes. Since then, I hadn't given them any reason to doubt me. The guys had doted on me like expectant fathers. But behind closed doors, they found every opportunity to make me moan and scream. Except for Jack.

This was the same Jack who'd gone out of his way to give me a small amount of time on Earth. He had let me show him all my favorite places. We were comfortable with each other now, so much so, we didn't think about it when we casually touched each other.

Sure, we had kissed and even had some heavy petting, but every time we came close to doing the deed, Jack pulled away. It made me wonder if it was me. I knew he could feel his desire for me. It pressed between my thighs while I sat on top of him. So, it couldn't be the lack of want. Maybe my father wasn't the only one who said something he really didn't mean. Did he not want to be with me because of Raiden and Firestar? He'd said he was okay with it, but maybe he'd only said it so I wouldn't turn him away. The very thought made my heart ache. I hated to have him with me and not be happy.

My eyes glanced to the side, seeking out Jack where he stared down at his salad, a pinch of skin sat between his eyes as if he were thinking hard about something. My hand slid onto his thigh, and I squeezed. Jack's ice blue eyes jerked up from his meal and met mine. The intensity there startled me.

Something was wrong. I opened my mouth to ask him what, but then snapped it shut. Now was not the time. Especially if what he had to say had to do with us and my lies. Couldn't have him airing our dirty laundry at the lunch table. If only everyone else at the table would learn to follow suit.

"How are you feeling, Maya? Any morning sickness?" My mother asked before taking a sip from her water glass. She might be as suspicious as my sister, but at least she seemed to be letting me figure it out on my own rather than prodding me with questions every moment of the day, making me feel even guiltier. I had lied about being pregnant.

"A bit," I muttered, turning my eyes back to my own plate. I was never good at lying to her, and she could tell right away every time I did. My father, on the other hand, didn't pay enough attention to me to know my eye color let alone if I was lying.

Speak of the dragon.

"Let's not talk about such things right now, I'm eating," My father, the Lord of Waesigar, said, clearly disgusted by the talk of my pregnancy symptoms. As if he wasn't the one pushing me to get pregnant in the first place.

"Lord Dannan," Raiden interjected. Bless his heart. "My brothers have sent word about more raids on our lands. Have you heard any news of them?"

"Oh, yes." My father turned his attention away from me and to my suitor. "I'd meant to speak to you about those. Your father must have his hands full dealing with raids on top of your brothers' fight for the throne."

While my father went on about the newest raids, I mouthed thank you to the black and white-haired lightning dragon. He winked in return.

Of all my suitors, Raiden was the easiest to get along with. From the beginning, we've had an intense attraction to each other, combine that with a personality that made it impossible to stay mad at him for long, well, it was easy to see why I enjoyed his company.

…And it didn't hurt he was a complete alpha in the bedroom.

When the lights went out, those playful eyes turned hard and controlling as he demanded my pleasure while rarely caring if he found his own. The very thought of it shot straight to my core, making me press my thighs together.

The chair next to me jerked back from the table, and Jack stood abruptly, making my hand fall from his lap. "Please excuse me, I have business to attend to. My lord, ladies?" He bowed slightly, and his eyes met mine briefly. The pain within them hit me like an arrow to the heart before he turned and walked away.

I sat there for a moment stunned by what I saw before I wiped my mouth and also stood from the table. My movement startled the others, the conversation died out as everyone's eyes turned to me. I couldn't be bothered by their questioning eyes, my own gaze following Jack's back.

"Maya? Is everything alright?" My mother's concerned voice pulled my attention. The look in her eyes made me straighten out, clearing my face of all expression.

Placing a hand on my forehead, I tried to sound exhausted. Though, it wasn't that hard to fake. "Just feeling a bit tired. I think I'll go lie down."

My mother nodded, though her eyes told me she didn't believe me. I didn't doubt she probably knew I was going after Jack but thankfully didn't voice her opinion to everyone else.

I glanced at both Raiden and Firestar who each waved me off with a knowing look. Hell, Firestar seemed more interested in his meal than our fourth member. I tried not to think much about that as I left the dining room to find Jack.

I checked his room first which had been moved closer to mine as well as the others. Better to have them close for when the baby came, was my mother's thought. I had been grateful because it made it easier to hide how hard we were working to get me pregnant. I rarely slept alone, but sadly it was never Jack.

I really needed to remedy that. While I had no reason to be so needy, the desire to have him in my bed was overwhelming. Maybe it was the thrill of the unknown that made me crave his touch so much. Would Jack be a patient lover? A dominating one like Raiden? I needed to know!

Stomping my foot in frustration, I realized the ice dragon wasn't in his bedroom. I frowned, staring at the empty room and wondering where he was. Had he gone to the gardens again? He often liked to go there to think...

Only, I hadn't any need as I passed by my room, I saw him lying in the middle of my bed. Unfortunately, he was fully clothed, and something about the look on his face told me that was unlikely to change.

"Jack," I said his name slowly as I walked toward the bed. His almost translucent hair created a curtain around his face, making it impossible to see his expression. "While I love the idea of you in my bed, I'm guessing this isn't a, um, social call. What's wrong?"

"How long do you expect us to keep up this

charade?" His voice though muffled by his hair, came out tortured and exhausted. I knew the feeling. Lying had never been my forte, and the guilt always ended up eating at me until I eventually gave in and told the truth. But this time I couldn't. It was imperative that my father didn't find out I'd lied. If he did, I was pretty sure Firestar would mysteriously disappear.

Worse, if he did find out, he wouldn't just blame Firestar or me, he would blame Raiden and Jack too. Both of them would be in danger of my father's wrath. That I couldn't have.

"It wouldn't be such a lie if you and I slept together," I suggested, my fingers tracing the design on the bedspread.

Jack scoffed his head angling toward me slightly. "And have our first time be tainted by the pressure of your father? No thank you."

"Then when do you think we'll be able to?" I asked, sitting next to him on the bed. "If one of the others gets me pregnant that solves only one problem, but then we would still have to pretend." I placed my hand on his leg and leaned forward so I could brush his hair away from his face, tucking it behind his ear so I could see his pale blue eyes. They were so full of anguish, my heart hurt even as

I told him the hard truth. "And then there will be no chance it will be yours."

"As if I have a chance now?" He shifted away from me his shoulders tense. "Raiden and Firestar are in your bed and between your thighs at every chance. I don't have much of a chance as it is."

I sighed as aggravation started to sink in. I wasn't going to feel guilty for having sex with the others. The whole point of this was to get me pregnant. It wasn't my fault Jack had hangups. I had tried my best to make sure they all felt equal. Even Firestar who had been against our foursome had come to share better than Jack did.

Instead of venting my frustrations out on him, I moved closer until I sat between his thighs. Then I wrapped my arms around his neck, my fingers tangling in his long, lustrous hair. "No one's between my thighs now." I coyly grinned. "It's a problem to be sure."

Jack opened his mouth, and for a moment, I swore he was going to push me away again, but then his arms wrapped around my waist and pulled me close.

"I suppose I will have to remedy that," he murmured, bringing his face to mine.

A brush of lips turned into a fight to breathe as

we tried to devour each other. I crawled up into his lap so that I straddled him, my lower half grinding against him. Jack grunted, and his hand clutched in my dark tresses, pulling me closer to him.

My hands pulled at his shirt, his usual suit jacket already tossed in a chair before I'd entered the room. I hurried to undo each button, but my over-excited fingers couldn't get them undone fast enough. With a twist of my wrist, I used my magic to pull the shirt open, causing a few of the buttons to pop off.

Jack pulled away from our kissing to frown at me. I smirked, daring him to chastise me but in an out of character move, he flipped us over, so my back pressed against the bed. Laughing, I wrapped my legs around his waist to keep him close.

My laughter died in my throat as my eyes met his exposed chest. Long lines of pale muscle showed through the flaps of his shirt, and my hands itch to touch him. Giving into the need, I traced my fingers along the contours of his chest, reveling in the hard strength beneath them. My fingertips trailed down his abs and along the line of pale hair ending at the top of his pants.

Locking eyes with Jack, I licked my lips before unsnapping his pants and reaching inside. I grasped him in my hand. Far thicker than the others, it was like warm steel wrapped in silk. The dragoness inside of me craved every last inch of it, but the other half of me wondered if he'd even fit.

"Don't worry, Maya. I would never hurt you." His words came out a breathy groan as he placed his hand on top of mine slid our hands together along his length.

I sat up on the bed, my hand still on his as my mouth sought his. Tongues tangling, Jack released my hand, and the coolness of his touch found my skin beneath the bottom of my shirt. I shivered but didn't pull away as the contrast of our temperatures nearly overwhelmed me with ecstasy.

Reluctantly I let go of Jack long enough for him to pull my shirt over my head, revealing my naked breasts since I'd neglected to wear a bra today.

The moment the cool air hit my nipples, they pebbled, but it was Jack's need that truly set me ablaze When Jack's eyes settled on them, his pale blue orbs filled with hot desire that warmed my skin.

Urging me onto my back, Jack slid down my skin with his lips while his hands went to my pants. His nimble fingers quickly untied my pants, dipping them inside briefly, teasing me so I squirmed on the bed.

Jack's mouth trailed along my stomach, and I arched up, making it easier for him as he pulled both them and my panties down my legs. Now completely bare to his view, insecurity filled me. Raiden and Firestar had never been quiet in their praises of my body, but Jack had a stoic way about him that made it impossible to tell what he was thinking.

Did he like what he saw? I didn't have full hips like many of my fellow dragonesses. My chest had always been smaller than most, along with my height. Men were rumored to love women of all kinds, but for some reason, Jack's attention to me often left me wondering how true that was.

He didn't say anything as his gaze swept across my skin. Heat filled my stomach even as my arms moved to cover myself. Jack's shot out to stop them, pressing them into the mattress.

"Don't," he growled, and all my uncertainty went away. That one word had so much need in it, I felt it all the way down to my core.

Breathing heavily, Jack released my hands and opened my thighs, exposing my slickened folds to his eyes.

This was it. We'd finally come together. I feared and craved it at the same time, my body a mixture of nerves and desire. I shut my eyes, waiting for him to enter me, but when he touched me next, it wasn't what I thought. His tongue slid across my most sensitive bits.

"Jack," I gasped, my hands reaching out to grab him as my eyes opened.

The ice dragon gave me a knowing smirk before delving back between my thighs. He didn't take his time, not like he did with everything else. Jack lapped and sucked at a feverish pace, shooting me higher and higher.

Breath coming out in pants, I reached down, entwining my fingers in his long hair. If he wanted to take me now, I'd be more than happy to comply, but Jack didn't seem to have any plans for completing what he started. As I screamed out my ecstasy and started to come back down, he moved beside me and laid on his side, his fingers stroking my skin.

"I love that I can cause you to make such sounds," he murmured his voice low and husky. "You're so needy. Wanton for my touch."

His words made my face heat before causing a defiant part of me to rear up. "You aren't the only one who can cause such sounds." Jack's brows furrowed as I moved between his thighs.

Giving him a little shove, I pulled his pants the rest of the way down his legs before staring at the beast beneath my hands.

Thick and long, it would be difficult getting him completely inside any part of me. Still, I was never one to back away from a challenge.

2

Jack grunted, his head thrown back as I slid my mouth over the end of him. The salty taste of him hit my tongue as I swallowed the tip of him. He jerked on the bed in response, urging me to take him further into my mouth.

I couldn't help but smile at his reaction. While the taste of him on my tongue made my own desire for him grow, it was nothing compared to hearing him cry out and beg me for release. Torturing him was definitely going to be my new favorite pastime given how he'd done nothing but drive me wild with lust for the last few weeks.

One would think if he was going to go through all the trouble of taking me on a romantic date on

Earth, he'd want something out of it. He'd let me drag him all over the city and even sat through a sappy romance movie. He'd logged more brownie points than any of the others, and I would have been happy to let him cash those in by the end of the evening. Hell, even before the movie was over.

But not Jack.

He'd been a perfect gentleman the entire time. Frustratingly so. Hell, when we climbed into the limo on the way home I launched myself at him. But even that had ended without sex. There was some deep kissing and heavy petting, but Jack shut it down before it could go any further.

I respected that he didn't want our first time to be decided by a lie to my father even though most men would have been happy to have an excuse to get me on my back. It made me want him even more, but there was only so much a woman could take. I was ready to explode!

A loud moan hit my ear, and my eyes shot up to Jack's face. He was close now. I'd ached to have him like this for weeks now. Sure, we'd almost gotten to this point several times but never so close as now. I hoped this time we could go all the way and I could finally know Jack completely.

It didn't hurt that it would fix one of my lies.

Who knew pretending to be pregnant was so hard? My mother fluttered around me like a worried hen, and my father boasted at every turn how he'd finally have a strong male heir to carry on our line. I didn't bother to mention that my child could very well be a girl. Instead, I focused on trying to get pregnant with the three supportive dragons who stood by me through all my dishonesty and craziness. Well two, anyway.

Irritation filled me, and this time, instead of helping Jack along to his release, I slowed down. I stroked him languidly, my hand reaching beneath to caress the sensitive sack beneath his length. Jack's eyes snapped open, and he stared down at me. I'd hoped getting him naked and excited would be enough to make him take the final step, but now I just wanted to torture him the way he had done me.

"Maya," Jack's voice came out raspy as his fingers tangled in my hair. He tried to move me faster, but I shook my head, releasing myself from his hold. "Please."

I almost relented at his pleading, but the pulsating ache between my thighs reminded me not to give in. I slid my mouth up and down him, moving at a glacial pace as I made the strong, stoic man before me toss and turn on the bed.

Still, my own desire was getting the best of me, keeping me from savoring each moment of our time together. I moved faster, making Jack cry out and causing my pride to swell. He grew and pulsated in my mouth, and while my own jaw ached from his girth, I knew he was almost there. Just a bit more.

As I prepared myself for Jack's release, someone pounded on the door. I froze in place, my eyes locking with Jack's as we both kept quiet. Maybe they would leave if we didn't answer.

"Hey, I was wondering if-" As the door swung open, Raiden's words died in his throat, his brown eyes quickly taking in the sight of me with my mouth still around Jack.

What a sight we must look. Jack spread out on my bed his chiseled chest bare and his pants still hanging off his feet. I sat between his thighs with my naked backside pointed toward the door. Raiden's eyes zeroed in on my nude form, and his tongue slid across his bottom lip.

I shifted in place, my desire easily seen decorating my inner thighs. My movement caused Raiden's nostrils to flare as he inhaled deeply. His eyes closed briefly before they opened once more, locking with mine, his face hardening into one I'd come to know so well.

"It seems I'm interrupting," he growled, a sound that resonated straight to my core. Part of me thought he would turn around and leave, embarrassed to have caught us in such a position, but I should have known better.

Raiden's demeanor changed, his usually relaxed shoulders stiffened, and his eyes narrowed as he shut the door and stalked toward us. A shiver rushed through me at his heated gaze. There was just something about his ability to switch from the life of the party to dominating alpha male in an instant that made me quiver.

"Please don't let me stop you," he said, stopping at the end of the bed. "Continue."

Raiden's words shouldn't have surprised me. He had made it clear he didn't mind sharing me any in any aspect, but still I hesitated. My gaze went to Jack whom I worried wouldn't be so nonchalant about it. Did it bother him? We hadn't exactly talked about us doing things with all of us. Only that they would share me. I didn't expect any of them to touch one another, whether they swung that way or not.

But I shouldn't have worried. Jack's eyes usually

cold as steel, liquefied with lust and seemed eager for me to take him back in my mouth even more so since Raiden watched us. A strange feeling filled me at the thought. Part of me found it taboo but at the same time excited for it to happen.

Still a bit unsure about having an audience, I slowly turned my back to Raiden. Nerves standing on end, my body a hundred percent aware of the lightning dragon's eyes on me. When I leaned back over and engulfed Jack's length once more, I could feel the Raiden's hot gaze between my thighs.

My body rigid with tension, I found it hard to find my rhythm with Jack once more. After a few moments of jerky movements, a hand placed on top of my head. I froze, my eyes shooting to Jack who only watched on with desire filled eyes, his hands firmly by his side. So, the hand on my head had to be Raiden's.

A second hand stroked my spine, and a cooing noise came from Raiden, urging me to relax. Easy for him to say. I'd never been with more than one man at a time. While I'd been happy to daydream about it even so far as to imagine all three of them taking me at once, being faced with it for real was an entirely different story.

With some effort, I let out a breath and tried to

keep from freaking out. It was fine. It couldn't be that different than being with only one of them, right? There were just more bodies to touch, more skin to pleasure, and more holes to take up. I swallowed deeply at the thought, forgetting for a moment that Jack was in my mouth until he groaned.

Raiden's hand on my head pressed down slightly, urging me to move. His other hand caressed my back as he guided me up and down Jack's length. I swallowed and locked my eyes with Jack, using him as a focal point as Raiden guided me. The hand on my back snaked lower, dipping between my cheeks and gliding against my folds. I jerked and sucked on Jack harder, pulling a sound from him as Raiden's long fingers found my core, pressing into me, stretching me until I felt a satisfying fullness.

His fingers moved inside me slowly before Raiden shifted his touch, pulling a muffled cry from me as he rubbed me in a new spot. I stopped moving over Jack, arching up in pleasure, only as I did, his fingers stopped as well. Worse, he didn't resume his ministrations until I returned my attention to Jack. I found it hard to concentrate on the task at hand with Raiden's fingers buried inside of me. Every time I stopped moving because the pleasure became too much, Raiden stopped as well, leaving me just on that edge and bursting to be taken.

When the lightning dragon's hand slid from my folds and moved up to settle on my hips, I tensed. I released Jack from my mouth and turned, but Raiden only shushed me, his fingers soothingly caressing my skin, turning me back. I let out a breath through my nose and moved my tongue along the bottom of Jack's length. I focused on the taste of his skin and sweat as Raiden shuffled behind me. The hard tip of him pressed against my heat and when he slid into me, I almost choked on Jack.

I breathed deeply through my nose as Raiden waited. Meeting Jack's gaze, I swallowed the taste of him on my tongue as I began to move again. An overwhelming feeling of fullness came over me, and I realized there was nothing to fear. They wanted me any way they could have me.

Raiden pulled out as I reached the tip of Jack. When I moved my mouth down his length, Raiden moved with me, hitting deep inside. The feeling of them both inside me one at once was exhilarating. My dragoness cooed within me, loving nothing more than having two strong men at her pleasure. She urged me to move faster, telling me to take what we wanted.

Increasing my pace, I took Jack deep into my mouth, stretching my mouth as far as it would go. My hand moved along the part of Jack I couldn't fit, my saliva dribbled out of my mouth, making movement easier. Raiden and Jack groaned together as Raiden pounded into me.

My jaw ached from keeping it open, but my need was too great to stop. Raiden's grip on my hips tightened as I increased my speed further, bobbing up and down on Jack's length. The ice dragon reached his release first. Jack filled my mouth, and I tried to swallow, but at that moment, Raiden hit just the right spot, making me scream.

My fingers dug into Jack's thighs as I tried to grab hold of the pressure exploding through me. I closed my eyes, my mind focused on what I felt while Jack's voice called out.

"Open your eyes." My eyes snapped open and locked with his pale orbs. Satisfied and spent, he watched my face as Raiden took me from behind. As I screamed my release until my throat hurt, it was Jack's face burned into my retina.

Raiden and I collapsed on the bed a moment

later, his slick front against my back. Our breathing heavy, we laid there for a few moments, basking in what just happened. My dragoness curled up inside of me sated and content.

"You don't seem tired to me."

All three of us jerked, our gaze going to the voice. My sister, Aeis, stood at the door completely unembarrassed by the sight of me with two men.

Raiden moved off me, pulling his pants up as he handed me Jack's discarded shirt, which I pulled over my head. Jack sat up and grabbed his pants still at his ankles, his eyes downcast. Out of the three of my suitors, Jack seemed the most skittish about sex and public displays of affection, so I wasn't surprised by his embarrassment.

Raiden on the other hand just went with the flow. Proud of his looks and not ashamed to flaunt them, he gave my sister a pleased grin before looking to Jack. "Let's go see if the cook has anything left over from lunch. I'm suddenly starving." He winked at me before nodding to my sister as he passed by.

Jack stopped at my side, he brushed his knuckles against the side of my face. I smiled up at him and inclined my head slightly.

When my sister and I were alone, my smile fell.

"What do you want, Aeis?" I turned from her and walked into the bathroom, not caring if she followed or not. I found a washcloth and wetted it in the sink.

"I want to know what the hell is going on," my sister snapped from the bathroom door. She crossed her arms over her chest and leaned against the frame as I lifted my leg to wash beneath Jack's shirt.

"I don't know what you are talking about," I muttered, not meeting her eyes.

"Bullshit."

My head jerked up at her curse. My sister rarely uttered a dirty word. She thought it would make her seem less ladylike. I'd never had that problem.

Dropping my leg down, I tossed the washcloth into the sink. "Is that what you think?"

Aeis came into the bathroom and stopped inches from me. "I think you need to learn to lie better."

I swallowed but didn't drop my gaze. Until she flat out said it, I wouldn't admit to anything. I might not like to lie, but the fewer people who knew the truth, the better.

"How long do you think you can keep this up?" Aeis asked when I didn't answer. "Eventually they will expect you to start showing, and you won't be fooling anyone in those clothes." She picked at Jack's shirt with interest. "You should start wearing looser clothing. It will hide it longer."

After giving her advice, she stepped back. Aeis glanced at me for another moment before going to the door. She paused there and said, "You're lucky, you know."

"How so?" I cocked my head to the side.

Instead of answering, she said, "I understand why you did what you did. Why you still do even, but those men care for you. Don't let your anger against father destroy what you have with them. Some of us aren't so lucky."

I waited to see if she had anything else to say but she only sighed and fluffed her skirts. "Get cleaned up. Dinner will be ready soon."

3

I stepped into the shower, letting the hot water fall over my body like a calming balm to my frazzled nerves. My hair plastered to my face and shoulders, the brown color turning almost black as it wet. I'd let it grow out after I'd been banished. No reason to keep it short. No fights to fight. At least not any real ones. Which made it hard to distract myself from my fate.

I had to give it to the humans. They did know how to distract themselves from the world around them. So, absorbed, they wouldn't notice the house burning down around them until the roof landed on their head.

Unfortunately, I didn't have that pleasure. Even working on the Waesigar video game with Ryan I had a hard time losing myself in the game world. It was all too real. Too much of a reminder of what I'd lost.

That wasn't the case now. Instead, as I looked around the real world of Waesigar, the one I used to cry for at night while I lay in my human apartment, I felt conflicted.

My head still told me to run back to Earth. To find a portal and run as fast and as far as I could until I was lost in the human world. There were enough humans there that I could go to any part of the world, and my father wouldn't be able to find me.

Yet...

And yet, my heart wouldn't let me.

I had come back to Waesigar on my father's request. I'd met his suitors and gone on his quest all the while plotting how to get out of it all. But along the way, something had happened. The suitors I had only meant to pretend to get along with, somehow wiggled their way inside of me. Now, their claws hooked so far into me, the very thought of running from them made my heart ache.

Nevertheless, my feelings wouldn't mean crap, if my father found out I lied. My sister knew. No doubt, my mother knew as well. It would only be a matter of time before my father figured it out.

I placed my hand on my flat stomach. My sister was right. They would be expecting me to start showing soon. I had few choices to hide what I'd done. Wearing looser clothing was a solution but only a temporary one. I had to get pregnant, but dragons had a notoriously hard time getting pregnant, it might still take years.

The best option would be to leave.

My stomach jumped at the thought. West Waesigar was not my home anymore. Not while my father reigned. He would continue to berate me for laying with all three of them even though he had been the one to suggest it in the first place. Worse, Firestar had been mocked nearly every time he was in the same room with my father, and I knew his patience was dwindling.

As I rinsed the soap from my hair, the shower door burst open. Cool air hit my naked body, and I shifted into a defensive stance. One foot back and my fists up in front of me. I readied myself to strike out, but then a head of fiery red hair came into view. I rarely had alone time and seeing Firestar caused irritation to prick at me, but the other part relieved it was someone I knew.

"Firestar," I breathed, relaxing my stance. His large frame filled the shower door, his muscles covered with brown sludge. Wrinkling my nose, I laughed, "What happened to you?"

Firestar's brows furrowed, his lips turned down in a frown. "That damned Raiden thinks he's so funny." He moved into the shower, and I shifted to let him underneath the water.

I forced back a laugh as I watched him scrub the mud from his skin. Picking up a washcloth, I began to wash his back. With a smile on my lips, I asked, "What did he do this time?"

A growl release from Firestar, rumbling beneath my hands. "We were blowing off steam training with the palace guards when he swiped my feet out from under me after we'd agreed to take a break. I swear he picked the biggest pile of slop to drop me in," Firestar snapped, his scrubbing becoming fiercer. "Do you think he makes me look the fool on purpose or just for his own idiotic pleasure?"

Frowning at his words, I urged Firestar to turn around. "I highly doubt Raiden thinks of anyone's amusement but his own. You are easy to prod at," I paused and then snorted, "Well, not as easy as Jack is, but either way, you shouldn't let him bother you so much."

"Raiden only messes with me because I've fucked you. Jack hasn't, so he's not as much of a threat." Firestar smirked, his hands going to my hips, his fingertips making circles on my skin. His touch caused a tingle that burned inside of me, but his words caused a different kind of guilty feeling.

"You are a rude man." I shoved at his chest, throwing his hands away from me. I moved toward the shower door, but Firestar's hand caught mine. I glared at him but waited.

"I'm sorry. I was only teasing." His fingers stroked mine as he clasped our hands together. Firestar stared at me that same look in his eyes that used to make me weak in the knees when I was a teenager. Now, it still made my knees weak, but it also made me want to smack him upside the head.

"You shouldn't tease like that," I grumbled. "This will only work with everyone working together. If you guys are constantly at each other's throats, how are you going to help me against my father?"

Firestar drew me to him, pressing our bodies together. My breasts brushed against his chest, and his hands settled low on my hips. Nose rubbing against mine in feather-light kisses, Firestar murmured low, "I would never let him hurt you."

"I know, but Aeis knows I lied." I placed my hands on his upper chest before sliding them around his neck. "It won't be long before my father realizes I'm not pregnant. Whether or not I've slept with Jack is irrelevant. If anything, he'd be glad for it."

"Why do you think that?"

"Because of who I picked to be my mates," I explained and then when Firestar only raised a brow added, "He'd have been fine if it had been one of the guys he'd picked, but then I added you…"

"And he'd be happier if I'd been the one to have not taken you yet," Firestar snorted. "And your father is a blind fool. He only sees what he wants to, just like my own. They focus too much on the past. On power that has long died. We are dragons, but we are also intelligent creatures. We are not all brawn and flame."

I chuckled. "Tell me about it." I laid my face against his chest and chewed on my bottom lip. "There aren't many people in Waesigar who think like you do."

"You'd be surprised by how many agree with me." Firestar leaned away from me, his hand tilting my chin up. "Enough to rally behind a true queen of dragons."

Firestar's words surprised me. I'd never thought I'd come back to Waesigar, let alone be in the running to take of the West. Now, Firestar believed I could be queen of them all. I wasn't sure how I felt about that. Terrified came to mind but at the same time a sort of strange excitement.

Smiling at him, we stood in the shower until the water ran cold, but I barely noticed. My body warmed by the thought of taking all that my father held dear and leaving nothing in return. Change was coming, and its name was Maya.

Dinner wasn't any more pleasant than lunch had been. In fact, it was worse.

My father had been drinking long before Firestar and I arrived, and as I entered the room, I found him stinking of Dragon's Tears, the alcohol of choice in Waesigar. My mother sat at his side, her brow furrowed. She never liked it when he drank. My father had never been the nicest person, but he was far worse when his mind was muddled with alcohol.

"There's my prized whore." He lifted his glass in the air as he laughed. "Come sit and tell us how my heir is doing."

I gritted my teeth, my hand clutching Firestar's arm. "How nice of you to ask about your grand-child, father."

"Bah," my father scoffed, drinking deeply from his cup. "I want to know if my investment will pay out, now that every dragon in Waesigar has dipped their stick in my daughter."

Anger burned in me, but before I could retort my three suitors stood from their seats. The fury in their eyes resonated in myself. Jack's icy demeanor melted away, and his lip curled as he bared his teeth at my father. Raiden's easy-going facade broke, his lightning crackling at his hands.

But no one's anger was worse than Firestar's. I could feel it running through his veins as my hand sat on his arm. The water we had showered in didn't hold a candle to the fire burning along Firestar's skin. My own anger pushed to the side, I focused on Firestar and keeping him from doing something we could not take back.

Tightening my grip on his arm, I gave him a warning look, but he didn't meet my gaze. His brown eyes had turned to burning coal as he glared at my father. Only one word came from his mouth. "Three."

"What?" my father asked, his eyes glazed over with drink. "What did you say to me, boy?"

Firestar stepped forward, placing his hands on the back of his chair. "Only three have had the pleasure of your daughter's company, not all of Waesigar."

My father snorted. "What's the difference? Three, ten, a hundred. As long as one of you give me an heir, it doesn't really matter, now does it?" He raised a brow as if daring Firestar to contradict him.

Before Firestar could respond, I came to his side. "I'm already pregnant so how many dragons I lay with is my business alone. Last time I checked, we were not a monogamous species and you can't damn me for something you asked me to do. Something that you have done, yourself." My eyes flickered to my mother's pained face, and I added, "In the past."

"Do you have a point, daughter? Or do I have to wait until my grandchild is born?" My father rolled his eyes and sighed.

I opened my mouth to snap back at him, but my sister beat me to it.

"Father," Aeis's voice rose to echo off the dining room's walls. "I am your daughter, am I not?"

"You know you are, Aeis." He sighed once more.

"And I once was your heir, was I not?" Her gaze focused on him with an amazing amount of restraint. She had always been better at holding her temper than me. Which was why she would be a better leader than I ever would.

"Obviously, my heirs wish to annoy me to an early grave." My father laughed and drank from his glass once more.

"God will it," Firestar muttered beside me. I jolted him in the side with my elbow and took a seat at the table. With the way things were going, I doubted I'd get to my food before it went cold, and I'd had quite enough of cold food.

Firestar followed my example as well as Raiden and Frost, who retook their seats. Everyone's attention turned to my sister, waiting with bated breath to see what she could possibly say to sway our frustratingly stubborn lord to stop hounding me.

"Then as your former heir, I would like to try to explain what kind of position you have put my sister in." Aeis gaze shot to mine briefly before going back to my father.

"By all means," my father gestured to her with his cup. "Do enlighten us."

"The stress of being your heir, to have to one day rule all that you have built can take its toll." My sister explained as the rest of us picked at our plates. "And do you think being with child would make this stress better or worse?"

My father opened his mouth to say God knows what, but my sister continued as if he didn't exist.

"It makes it worse." She growled, her eyes flashing a golden hue. "Each mocking comment behind one's back builds to an inky black sickness." She swallowed hard and shook her head, coming back to herself. "If you speak ill of your own daughter, what makes you think others won't? How will she ever keep hold of our legacy if they all think she's a dumb slut?"

"All right, all right. I get it," my father growled, filling his cup once more. His gaze locked with mine, and for the first time ever, he looked ashamed. "You hear anyone say such things to you, report it to me and I will cut their tongues out, you hear?"

I nodded, my eyes burning, and I stared down at my plate before I could cry. Firestar who sat at my side placed his hand on top of mine and squeezed it in reassurance. My gaze meets his, and my lips curled into a smile.

The rest of the dinner was quiet. We were all absorbed in our own thoughts, I supposed. I only really cared about what my sister was thinking. I would love to know what thoughts made her face darken that way. Why her words to defend me moved her so?

That was when I realized she hadn't been talking about me. Sure, she had been trying to defend me, but in her own way she was also telling our father she blamed him for her barren body. The curse of being the heir to his throne caused so much stress, it would make anyone's eggs shrivel up and die.

"I do have one question, Maya," my father said after a bit.

I forced myself not to sigh. This couldn't be good.

"And what's that?" I surprised even myself by how level my voice came out.

"When your child is born, how will you know the father?" My father held his cup to his mouth as the words came out. Then he took a long, slow drink.

If I thought the table had been quiet before, the

silence now was deafening. The clanking of silver-ware ceased. Not even the sound of each of us breathing could be heard.

It was a question I'd been asked before, and I doubted it would be the last time. It was also one I didn't have an answer for. If we were in the human world, we'd have done a DNA test to find the father, but I didn't dare suggest that to a room full of alpha dragons. Though, I felt my men might be a bit more likely to humor me.

As it was, my father wanted an answer I couldn't give. I had no idea what to say, and as his eyes bore into me waiting for my reply, I did the only thing I could do.

I placed the back of my hand to my mouth, my other hand going to my stomach as I pretended to lurch forward. Firestar touched my arm as I jumped to my feet as I said, "I think I'm going to be sick."

4

After leaving dinner, I went to the only place I ever truly felt at home. The gardens. Funny since while the castle was my home, my bedroom never gave me solace, only the large expansion of green which covered the whole of the back of the castle.

Rows and rows of flowers decorated the bushes that lined the walkways. They wound around in a path only those who had traveled it knew. A stranger would find themselves lost in moments, wandering for hours through the maze of greenery, wondering how to get out.

Not me. I spent more time here than I did in my own bedroom or even the training grounds. I knew the paths like the back of my hand. I could walk them with my eyes closed. Now, as I rushed away from my father and his many questions, I appreciated that ability, needed it.

The green passed by me in a blurred wave my feet pounding on the ground until I came to my favorite place in all the garden. A fountain of black marble, shaped in that form of a great dragon, its wingspan larger than mine would ever be even if I could conjure them. Better still was the bench beneath the dragon that allowed one to sit in the shadow of its greatness. It had always made me feel safe and secure. It was like the stone dragon had my back.

I needed its protection now more than ever. While, I knew each one of my men would stand up for me, maybe even die for me, if it came down to it, I couldn't let them fight all my battles for me.

My father, I could handle in most cases, but he was becoming more and more difficult with each day I stayed. It was as if my being pregnant made him more ashamed of me than when he banished me before. I didn't know if I could dodge his questions or his anger for much longer.

Outside the castle wasn't much better. From what I'd heard, there were more raids every week. If I left the safety of my father's home, I would face the dangers of Waesigar. Memories of the last attack when we had headed to the Southern Region filled my head. While Jack and Raiden had taken out more than their fair share of attackers, I had barely been able to fight off one.

"Such a weakling," I muttered to myself, glaring down at the stone path beneath the bench. I used to be a great fighter. One of the best in the Western lands, but five years away, and I'd become a weakling… especially compared to my suitors. I'd learned how to fight like a human, but the dragons who attacked me weren't going to wait around like Ned until I swept their legs from under their feet. The feet that hovered in the air as they sliced my head off from the sky.

"Can't say that I'm surprised to see you here."

My head jerked up at the sound of my cousin, Ned's, voice. Almost ten years older than me, he was war-worn and far more experienced in battle than I would ever be. He had my dark hair, but his eyes were golden where mine were as green as the surrounding garden. Ned wore his armor no matter where he went, the dining hall or the gardens, he was always ready for a fight.

"Hello, Ned." I tried to sound pleasant, but it only came out tired. I'd only seen my cousin in passing since I came back. Which surprised me since he'd been the one to bring me home in the first place.

Ned sat beside me on the bench, his leg warm against my own. "Your father being a right bastard as usual?"

I snorted at Ned's description. Only someone who had grown up with my father lording over them would dare say such a thing about the Lord of the West, in private or not.

"When is he not?" I asked and then sighed, staring down at my laced fingers.

"He wasn't always like this you know," Ned informed me, leaning back against the fountain, so the sound of the water muffled most of his words.

"Really?" I cocked a brow, finding it hard to believe my father had not always been an asshat. "He was nicer? He couldn't possibly have been any worse. Though," I chuckled. "He is getting up in the years, maybe being senile has made him more tolerant."

Ned laughed beside me. "Lord Dannan? Senile? That's as likely as the stone dragon coming to life right here in this very garden." He gestured behind us to my silent protector, its eyes, and teeth fierce in their frozen expression.

I gave a halfhearted laugh. "Yes, I suppose you are right."

We sat in a companionable silence for a few moments before Ned placed his hand on mine. Confused by the sudden affection, I stared up at my cousin with raised brows.

Ned's own face had sobered, his forehead drawn down and a darkness moved behind his eyes. "I can't say that I don't agree with him though."

"What do you mean?" I asked and tried to move my hand away, but Ned held tight, pinching my fingers together.

"You were supposed to be the answer to it all. The great heir to save the day." He shook his head and sighed. "But you have disappointed us. Me most of all."

"I don't know what you are talking about," I growled and jerked my hand from his grasp. I stood and began to walk away. If he was going to ask me more questions, criticize my decisions, I didn't want to hear it.

"Lying to the Lord of the West is a crime punishable by death," Ned called out after me. "Even if you are his daughter."

Pausing mid-step, I slowly turned back to him.

"Then it's a good thing I haven't lied, isn't it, cousin?"

Ned's expression changed to something I'd never seen before. A cruel sort of smile crawled up his face and his eyes filled with righteous glee. "What will he say I wonder, when he finds out you aren't pregnant? Maybe he will claim you are barren as well and name someone else heir. Someone worthier of the position."

His words caused a suspicious feeling to settle into my gut. If I were found barren like my sister, Aeis, the next member in line would be Ned himself. My father wasn't the only one I had to worry about now.

"Or better yet," Ned continued, standing from the bench. "If that someone else already had a pregnant mate when they told Lord Dannan of his own daughter's deceit." He placed his hands behind his back and stood a few feet away from me, his eyes boring into me. "I would think, our lord would be very grateful in his praises, don't you?"

Anger and confusion filled me. Ned was someone I thought had been on my side. He'd never been unkind to me growing up and it had been him who my father had trusted to bring me home. Which didn't make sense why now, he has decided to turn on me.

"And you think my father will just hand the kingdom over? To you?" I scoffed, shaking my head. "How do you know he'll even believe you?"

"That's a fair point. Your father has been known to ignore reason for power," Ned said, and the look in his eyes made me take a step back. "Maybe, I'll just kill you and get it over with. Then it won't matter what he chooses to believe."

"I thought you wanted me here. You practically begged me to come," I snapped, reminding Ned of when he had come to collect me.

He'd told me they needed me. I was the only one who could make all the old generation see that change was needed for us to survive. Ned had even gone so far as to threaten violence to make me come back. I should have taken that threat as a signal of something else entirely.

"You're right, I did." Ned's eyes narrowed, anger sparking within them. "That was before I knew you'd take that hothead to your bed. That was a poor choice in a string of poor choices."

"What does that have anything to do with it," I countered. How many people were against me just because I took Firestar to my bed? Would they all be like Ned and think it would be better for me not to be the heir as long as I had Firestar at my side?

"You've been gone a long time, Maya. How do you know what any of us are like?" Ned stepped uncomfortably close to me. Something in his expression made a chill run through me as he placed his hands on my shoulders. "It's not even that." He met my eyes and there was something in them I'd never seen before. Lust. "I honestly thought you'd pick me, but ever since you got here, you haven't even looked at me." His lips turned into a cruel smile. "Don't you remember what you said when we were kids? How you wanted to marry me?"

I swallowed hard, forcing back disgust. What Ned was suggesting wasn't just vile but forbidden. Multiple partners of either sex was completely acceptable but to lie with one's family member - even a cousin - would be the deepest of depravities. Sure, as a kid, I hadn't known better, and neither had he, but now?

I shook my head, trying to banish the though. The fact that my cousin had even suggested it showed how right he had been in his words. I didn't know him at all.

"Unhand me, Ned." My voice was hard, and I shook with anger at his very touch.

"Is that really what you want, Maya?" he insisted. "Even now, you need a strong man, one with strong genes to provide you an heir. You need me." As he spoke, I drew upon the earth around me, my magic pulling at the roots beneath the bushes. When he leaned toward me, his eyes closing as if to kiss me, the roots shot from the ground and smashed into the back of Ned's knees.

Shock filled his face as his legs collapsed beneath him, but he didn't release my shoulders. We both ended up on the ground, but the moment I hit the stone, I scrambled away from him. His hand grabbed my ankle, his nails biting into my skin, drawing blood. I cried out as pain shot through my leg.

I kicked with my other leg, hitting him in the shoulder and then the side of the head. I aimed for his face as I tried to focus my magic on coming to my defense once more. The roots wrapped around his legs and pulled him the opposite direction, but Ned held fast to my ankle, dragging me with him.

My magic was strong. I'd practiced it for years and had been at the top of my class, but I'd been gone for too long - too out of practice. Nevertheless,

Ned was not. His magic came swift and brutal, ripping apart the roots I had taken as my own. In a matter of seconds, I found myself flat on my back with my cousin's enraged face staring down at me, his own roots holding me down.

"Not so strong without your suitors, now are you?" Ned growled in my ear, the feel of his breath hot against my neck made my stomach roll. "It's time you found out exactly what a real man is like."

When Ned's hand found its way between my thighs, my inner dragon roared in protest, she did not like this coward of a dragon who would take a female against her will let alone one he called family.

His eyes roamed over my body, and I struggled against my binds tenfold. I didn't like him touching me. I wanted to dig my claws into his face, pluck the eyes that imagined me naked from his eyes. My dragoness growled her approval, urging me to shed blood and plenty of it.

As power roared up in me and the earth started to respond to my call, Ned was snatched from me and thrown across the walkway. I didn't see where he landed, but the thud had a satisfying crunch to it that made me swell with glee. A crackling sound filled my ears before my binds were broken and my eyes found my savior.

Raiden stood above me, tall and full of fury. His trident held in his hand, lightning crackled around him until he was almost encompassed by it. If I ever met a thunder god, I'd imagine he would look the way Raiden did right now - powerful, terrifying, and hotter than the seventh level of hell.

"Are you all right?" My lightning god offered me his hand, and for a moment, I hesitated afraid the light covering his body would hurt me. Then I shook the fear away, Raiden wouldn't hurt me, and if he wouldn't, his magic wouldn't. I slid my hand into his, the crackling light engulfing my hand like a warm caress.

Pulling me to my feet, Raiden held me to his side while pointing his trident toward where Ned had begun to crawl to his feet. Blood trickled from a cut on Ned's lip, making the snarl on his face even more fearsome. His eyes flickered to Raiden's trident, worry in his expression before the roots began to slither beside him.

"How dare you attack me," Ned sneered. "Don't you know who I am, or are the dragons in your region too stupid to care?"

Raiden's grip on my shoulders tightened, his

eyes hard and fierce. "I know who you are, but the question is. Why were you attacking your own cousin? Do you have a death wish?"

"Watch your mouth boy," Ned snapped, stepping toward us, his roots slapping the ground violently. "You may very well be speaking to the next Western Lord."

"That will never happen," I jumped in, but before I could say more, Raiden's hand on my shoulder stopped me. My eyes stayed on Ned as my dragoness filled the forefront of my mind. An unrecognizable emotion flittered over Ned's face, and I knew that my eyes had gone gold like my inner dragon. A low rumble came from my throat as I growled, "If you ever touch me again, I will cut your hands off and feed them to you. Do you understand?"

Ned face contorted like he had swallowed something nasty. He nodded. He shifted as if to leave but stopped. "This isn't over. I won't let someone unworthy sit on the throne." He promised before he turned on his heel and stomped away.

My shoulders fell, and I sighed. Like my life wasn't already complicated enough. I'd have understood if Ned just wanted to get rid of me and my supposedly bad choices but to want to impregnate me himself? I shuddered at the thought.

"What happened?" Raiden turned me in his arms, his face full of concern but also an underlying anger. I didn't blame him. If he hadn't shown up, I couldn't bear to think of what could have happened.

"Ned knows I'm not pregnant. Which just means it's only a matter of time before everyone else finds out." I shook my head, panic slowly making its way into my chest. "I don't know what to do."

"It'll be okay," Raiden assured me with a soft smile and then frowned. "Do you know why he suddenly attacked you?"

I frowned hard, not wanting to bring the words to life. "Ned thinks I made a mistake adding Firestar to my bed."

Raiden's fingers tightened on my arms, and his eyes narrowed. "And let me guess, he thought he was a better choice?" I nodded and swallowed thickly. Raiden's face softened, and he pressed his face to my hair, inhaling deeply. "You shouldn't have gone by yourself. If I hadn't been here to stop it…"

"But you were," I interrupted. "How did you find me, anyway?"

He leaned away from me and smirked, "Don't you think I have your scent down by now? I could find you if I were blind and deaf."

"That's good to know." I chuckled nervously, my mind sobered with what happened and what we should do next. I knew what I wanted to do, but I didn't exactly know how to go about it or if the guys would want even to.

As if reading my mind, Raiden murmured, "Firestar told me you want to leave." I stared up at him, waiting to find out what he thought of it. Would he tell me I was a coward? That I should stay and deal with my lies, and now Ned, who was gunning for me. "I agree."

My eyes jerked up at his words. "You do?"

Sighing, Raiden ran a hand through his hair. "It's becoming harder and harder to keep this lie going. And I don't like how your father is handling it. Add your cousin to the mix. It would be better for everyone if we left."

Chewing on my lip, I struggled to find a reason to disagree. "But where would we go?"

A knowing smirk covered Raiden's lips. "It just so happens my father has requested my presence."

Before I could ask why, Raiden continued with a less than happy tone. "It seems my brothers are going to start a civil war if someone doesn't intervene."

"Playing mediator is better than being here, I'm sure," I muttered, surprising even myself. I hated to be in the middle. Even on Earth, I hated being stuck between my friends, Ryan and Bianca. They were constantly arguing over what movie to watch or who had the better music collection. It could get to epic proportions which sometimes ended in neither of them talking to each other for weeks. I couldn't imagine being stuck between two warring princes. It would be a billion times worse than fighting over what to have for dinner.

"You say that now, but you haven't met my family." Raiden chuckled. "They might not be as intense as your father nor crazy as your cousin, but they have their own quirks that might make you take back those words."

I shrugged. "How far away from here is it?"

"Two-week carriage ride, five days if we fly."

"Perfect." The more distance between my family and myself the better.

5

The wind whipped my hair around me as I held onto Firestar's neck. His fiery wings beat close to my face, and I would have thought it'd be hot, but I barely felt any difference in temperature. The same went for the others. Each of them had taken turns carrying me since I still hadn't earned my wings. At this rate, I wondered if I'd ever get them.

It was all so unfair.

I screw them, and they get a power boost. I still wasn't really sure how that worked. Maybe a convergence of our powers as we made love? Some of our lore claimed that sex was like giving a part of your soul to the other person. If that were it, I wasn't so sure I cared for that. I was the one doing all the giving, how did that make sense? I was the one putting out, shouldn't I get something out of it? What was the point of having a magic vagina if it didn't give me my wings?

I sighed.

"What's wrong?" Firestar asked, taking his eyes from the sky in front of us. One good thing about flying was that you didn't have to worry about tripping or running into anything. Not unless it was a mountain, and the likelihood you'd run into one of those was slim to none.

"Don't you get tired of carrying me?" I asked, shifting in his arms to find a more comfortable position. Though, I shouldn't have bothered. There really was no comfortable position cradled mid-air. It was a good thing I wasn't afraid of heights anymore, or this would have been bad.

"Not really. I don't mind having you this close to me. At least, I know you won't twist your ankle." Firestar grunted. "Why? Does it bother you?"

"Do you think I'd be asking if it didn't?" I raised a brow at him.

"Don't tell me you'd rather walk? It'd take weeks to get to Raiden's home, and I, for one, don't want to spend that amount of time in the woods. I had enough of that back home." He frowned, and I didn't need to ask to know that he was thinking about his time back in the camp. Thinking about all those angry men we left behind, especially the way they'd acted when they found out I could give them powers, made my stomach knot. I could see how Firestar wouldn't want to be reminded of it, I sure as hell didn't.

"I'm not saying that," I finally said. "I'm just tired of being the weakling in the group. I can't fly. My fighting is subpar at best."

"But you were on Earth, it's understandable you'd be out of practice." Firestar readjusted his hold on me and signaled to Jack and Raiden, who trailed behind us, to come closer.

"That was Earth, this is Waesigar. I can't have you guys by me all the time. I must be able to protect myself better than I do now. Or more people will try to take advantage of me."

"Like your cousin, Ned?" Firestar growled, his teeth bared to a feral sneer.

"You told him about what happened?" I asked Raiden when he came into view.

He didn't even pretend to feel guilty. "Of course, I did. We all need to know our enemies, and your cousin has now put himself at the top of that list."

"Exactly," Firestar agreed. "My father might be a thief, but at least he isn't deranged."

"Which is exactly why I should know how to defend myself," I countered. "Raiden almost didn't make it to me in time."

"I agree with Maya," Jack said from the other side. "We should be focusing more on her training and less on getting her pregnant. There won't be any point in it if she's dead."

"Very well." Firestar nodded toward the ground. "There's a good place as any to make camp. We can start your training now."

"Now?" I gaped.

"Yes," Firestar locked his eyes with me as he began to descend. "We are going into a warring land, who knows what we will come up against."

I'd wanted to become stronger, but I didn't expect them to agree so quickly or want to start right away. I'd thought my suitors would be like my misogynist father and demand they be at my side all the time. The three of them never ceased to surprise me.

We landed with a thud in a small clearing that smelled of fish and trees. A stream or pond had to be near. It'd been a few days since I'd had a bath. Even a cold one was better than none, and if I was lucky, I'd get to see all three of my men shirtless and dripping wet.

"Later." Firestar growled in my ear, his hands caressing me as he sat me down. I blushed as I realized he'd probably smelled my arousal. Moving away from him, I kept my eyes on the surroundings and not on my other suitors who had no doubt picked up on it as well.

The clearing wasn't huge. We'd have enough room to sleep and make a fire, but that was about the extent of it. Fighting was out of the question.

"How do you propose we do this?" I asked, turning back to the three of them. "There's not enough room to do any kind of sparring."

The guys exchanged a look before Jack stepped forward. "Did you have much room to fight when your cousin cornered you?"

"No." I frowned. The area with around the dragon fountain was nothing more than a walkway. Not much room for fighting there either.

"That's because most of those who will attack you will do it where you can't run," Jack explained. "So, the best way to learn to fight off an attacker like your vile cousin is to pretend you are in a situation where you can't run away."

It made sense, but I didn't see how they could

teach me that. Then again, I didn't really have the time to think about what to do when Ned attacked. Probably because I never expected it. He'd always seemed like a good guy. Maybe a bit intense, but not someone who would try to violate his own family.

"Okay," I slowly drew out. "What do you want me to do?"

Firestar came forward with a slight grin on his face. "Turn around. I want your back to me."

Frowning at his command, I did what he said. "How am I going to fight you this way?"

"Do you think they will fight fair?" Firestar asked as he stopped behind me. He was so close, I could feel his body heat against me. My eyes sought out the others who had set our bags down and waited on the sidelines. Their eyes were firmly on Firestar and me.

"I already know how to fight," I reminded him over my shoulder. "I'm just out of-"

"Practice," Firestar finished for me. "Yes, I know, and the only way to get better is to practice. Now, prepare yourself."

I shifted my stance ready for him to come at me. In a battle, I wouldn't have time to think about how he would attack. I'd have to let my instincts figure it out and just act.

Without warning, Firestar grabbed me by the waist and dragged me to the ground. I didn't have time to think about how to stop him before he had me pressed to the ground. He shoved his hips against my backside grinding into me. I had a hard time focusing on the fact that we should be training, and not ripping of our clothes to mate.

Firestar's hands held my wrists on the ground as he murmured in my ear, "See how easy it was to get you in a compromising position? I could take your right now before you could stop me."

I swallowed hard as he ground into me once more before getting up. I crawled to my feet and stood in the same position as before. This time, when Firestar came at me, I shoved my elbow into his stomach, whipped around to kick him, but he effortlessly caught my leg.

Twisting around, I lashed out at him with my elbow as I fought to get my leg out of his hold. He blocked my blow before burying his hand into my hair and jerked backward so that my neck strained. I struggled to keep my balance as he shifted us into an even more awkward position. Firestar's hand on my leg slid up, making me roll my eyes.

"Really?" I asked turning my head to shoot him an annoyed look. "You can't train without coping a feel?"

Firestar smirked, his fingers stroking up and down the inside of my thigh. "What can I say, I never waste a chance to touch a beautiful woman."

I blushed and glanced down before peeking back up at him from beneath my lashes. With a coy grin, I puckered my lips as if to offer him my mouth, but when he came closer, I used his hold on me as momentum to throw my other leg up and over, driving my knee into the side of his head.

He stumbled sideways, losing his grip on my leg and causing me to crash to the ground. My shoulder ached from the impact, but I ignored it as I hurried to stand. Only, instead of attacking me, Firestar rubbed the side of his face and grinned.

"Good, you're learning." He shook his head and spun his finger in the air. "Turn around and let's do it again."

I sighed but did what he said. I listened for Firestar's heavy footsteps and waited to see what he would do next.

Firestar's hands came out from behind me, and I expected them to grab me and throw me to the ground. That wasn't what they did. They came up and cupped my breasts.

"Firestar, what are you doing?" I froze in place not sure what to do. "If you keep groping me, we won't ever finish practicing."

"Who said we weren't finished?" Firestar growled in my ear, his hands squeezing my chest. His fingers plucked at my nipples, causing a blast of pleasure to shoot through me.

"That's enough of that," Raiden interrupted, approaching us from the sidelines. "Let's see what our new powers are really made of."

Distracted by Raiden's interruption, Firestar let his guard down enough for me to launch my elbow back hitting him in the stomach. I twisted around and grabbed his arm, flipping him over and onto the ground with a loud thud. Groaning on the floor, I smirked down at him.

"Now, we are done."

Raiden burst out laughing while Jack chuckled politely on the sideline.

Firestar coughed and crawled from the ground. Drawing on his magic, Firestar's kusarigama, two scythe-like swords formed in his hands. Then without warning, he charged at Raiden.

Raiden's trident appeared with within seconds,

he must have been practicing on his own to make it form so quickly. He blocked Firestar's attack with his trident, a smirk on his lips. "Don't strain yourself now, Firestar." Firestar snarled and threw himself away from the lightning dragon.

Firestar and Raiden moved into position. Then as if rehearsed, they came at each other. Their weapons locked against each other, flames and lightning met causing a spectacular display of color. They were as evenly matched as they had been back in Firestar's camp. Each time one of them lunged the other dodged, Raiden was quicker, but Firestar put far more strength behind his hits. Soon the fighting took to the air. Once more a pang of envy filled me. If I could fly, then I wouldn't be such an easy target. Plus, escaping would be a piece of cake.

"Don't worry, Maya," Jack said from my side, patting my hand. "You will fly one day, I know it."

"How?"

Jack cupped the side of my face his fingertips stroking my cheek. "Because no one in this world deserves it more."

Before I could answer him, Raiden and Firestar broke apart with a yell. My gaze found them again and watched as they descended from the sky. They were both heaving in lungfuls of air, but they seemed thoroughly happy with the outcome of their match. Something I had missed.

"You are doing well with your new gifts," Jack said when they finally came back down to the ground. "Our enemies won't stand a chance."

"What about you?" Raiden asked as he wiped his face with the back of his arm. "You must have some badass powers now that you and Maya have been together."

Jack went silent, his eyes going down to the ground at Raiden's words. I knew why he didn't answer. It was because he didn't have any new powers yet. We hadn't had sex so there was no way he'd have gained any. Not unless oral sex counted, and I was pretty sure it didn't.

"I can't," Jack answered finally.

"Why not?" Firestar prodded, moving toward him his kusarigamas twirling in the air. "Don't tell me you're afraid?"

I could clearly tell their teasing bothered Jack. I really shouldn't feel bad for him. It was his fault we hadn't taken the last step yet. I thought we would finally do it last time, but then Raiden had stepped in. A delightful quiver ran through me, remembering how that ended, until remembered the problem that resulted.

Teeth gritted, I stepped up next to Jack. I couldn't keep the irritation out of my voice as I stated, "Because, we haven't had sex yet."

"What?" Raiden practically shouted. "How the hell is that possible?"

"Ask him." I crossed my arms over my chest and nodded toward Jack who had gone silent.

"I'm not surprised," Firestar said, rubbing his kusarigama s together with a nonchalant expression. "Jack doesn't seem like the kind of guy who can put his pride aside for those he loves."

"Not like you?" I quipped and snorted. "And what exactly would you call what you did when my father told us you would never be my husband?"

While I was frustrated by Jack's refusal to consummate our relationship, Firestar had no room to talk about putting aside one's pride. He'd done a fine job showing me that when we were teens.

"That was different." Firestar gave me a look. "This isn't about marriage it's about sex. Hot, sweaty, sex that will help get us out of the tight spot you put us in."

My lip puffed out in a pout as I realized he was right. It was my fault we even had to force Jack to be with me, and I knew that's not how I wanted it to be. Even worse for Jack to feel like he had to be with me because of my mistakes, but I wanted to be close to him. Like I was with the others. It didn't hurt that it would bring more power to our little foursome, and we needed all the help we could get.

"Fine," Jack snapped, jerking me from my thoughts. "If you feel that way then let's deal with this now."

I stared at him my mouth agape. "What are you saying?"

Jack stepped up to me until I could feel his breath on my face. "I'm saying, I'm going to fuck you. Right here, right now."

6

Jack's words had a visceral effect on my body. My thighs pressed together, trying to appease the throbbing need in my core. I was sure the three of them could sense my arousal even without my moments.

"Come on, Raiden," Firestar waved a hand over his shoulder. "Let's check out this water source, see if it's worth bathing in."

Raiden looked over to Firestar. "But don't you want to watch?"

The fire dragon rolled his eyes and grabbed Raiden by the arm. "You can watch all you want later. You didn't have anyone to watch your first time, did you?"

"That was different," Raiden argued, his eyes

on us Firestar led him away. "We weren't sharing her then."

"So, they don't need you nosing in. Let Jack and Maya have their time alone." Firestar nodded to Jack as he gave Raiden a good shove in the other direction. When Firestar and Raiden were out of earshot, my nerves began to take over.

"Uh, so." I let out a nervous chuckle. "Alone at last."

"Yes," Jack stated, his gaze turning to me. What I saw there made my foot step backward. I knew he wanted me, but right now, I also knew he was angry with me. Upset that I forced his hand, that I let out our little secret to the rest of the group. But it had to be done.

"Maybe we should set up camp first," I suggested, scanning the area for our bags. None of us had paid them any mind once we got there. Too absorbed in the promise of letting off steam. Now we would be doing it a different way.

"Why?" Jack asked. "Don't you want me to take you in the dirt like an animal? That's what you seem to think we are."

"No, I don't." I shook my head and held my hands up in front of me to ward him off. "I don't think that at all."

"Then what do you think?"

I chewed on my bottom lip as I tried to find an answer. I wanted Jack. I'd been the one who had pushed him to this with no regard for what he was really feeling, of course, he must think I thought nothing of sex. That it meant nothing. But he was very wrong.

While banished to Earth, I could have slept with any number of humans. No strings attached no chance of procreation. Dragon shifter and human DNA did not mix. I wasn't like the majority of my kind humans didn't attract me, but that wasn't what had kept me from mating with one of them.

It was my heart. I'd already given it away to Firestar to have it ripped from my grasp by my father. So, I spent the first few years of my banishment nursing those wounds. By time I came back to Waesigar, I'd already decided to make the next time I mated with someone to make it count.

Then that all went to hell when I practically rolled over and spread them for Raiden. I'd like to say I had more self-control than that, but I had shamefully given in to my baser instincts. Though, now I didn't feel so bad about it. Raiden was a good guy and a good choice for a father. And Jack would be too. But not if he was conflicted like he seemed.

"We should talk about this first," I suggested before I tripped over something on the ground and fell onto my butt. Before Jack could pounce on me, I scurried to my feet, my eyes never leaving him. He removed his jacket and folded it over his arm before thinking better of it and tossing it aside. I followed his fingers as he pulled his shirt out of his pants and began to unbutton the buttons. As each one popped open revealing a new expansion of skin, I couldn't help but lick my lips at the sight.

"No, I don't want to talk. I want to put to rest these mocking words. It is far past time in any case." He kept coming toward me as I walked backward. I felt like prey beneath his heated gaze, both afraid and aroused.

"But you must have a reason not to want to do it. Besides my father," I stuttered, trying to find some way to make him slow down. I didn't want our first time to be because he was trying to prove something but because he wanted to.

Jack frowned, his brow furrowing. "How is it you know how I feel?"

"Because usually when a guy says no, it's for a good reason, and my father is hardly a good reason," I pointed out, taking another step back from him.

The ice dragon quieted as his expression grew thoughtful. Then he sighed and flicked his hair behind his shoulder in a wave of icy blond. "You are right."

I sighed more relieved than I expected. "Then what is it?"

"The truth is," Jack started as he approached me. "I've never felt this way about any of my previous lovers."

I watched his face as I asked, "What way is that?"

Jack's pale eyes filled with emotion as he stopped before me. He picked my hand up and placed it on his chest, the pounding of his heart beating beneath my palm. "Every time I see you, my heart swells, and all thoughts leave my mind."

"Oh, that," I breathed my own heart speeding up at his words, but Jack wasn't done yet.

"Or," he continued, drawing my hand down his chest and across his abdomen to stop just above his pants. "I want you so much, I can hardly stand to be in the same room with you without my dragon demanding I take you."

My breath caught, and I swallowed thickly as he moved my hand lower to rest on the hard front of his pants. I'd already seen and tasted Jack quite thoroughly, but still, the feel of him made my pulse race and my mouth dry. Was I finally going to find out what it felt like inside of me? Would he even fit?

"Those are very good reasons," I responded, clearing my throat. "Reasons that should be respected and not rushed."

"Really?" Jack cocked his head to the side. "Because most would say those are reason enough to take you right now without guilt or regret." His hands wrapped around my waist and pulled me to him. My breasts brushed against his chest, and I couldn't breathe. "Unless..." he trailed off.

"Unless?"

"Unless, those feelings aren't reciprocated." He arched a brow an expectant look on his face.

That was when it clicked in my head. I knew what he wanted from me.

I quickly removed my hand from his pants and stared at him for a long, hard moment.

Jack wanted to know if I felt the same way about him. The problem was, I couldn't honestly make any declarations of love because I didn't know for sure how I felt about any of them. Even when it came to Firestar who had my heart before I had met any of the others, I was all twisted up inside. Could I really love three men at once?

Yes, yes, I could. But accepting it was a whole other thing.

Everything we had gone through, my family, Firestar's family, Jack and Raiden had stood by me the whole time without complaint. Even Firestar jumped at the chance to be with me once more although I had two other men vying for my attention. It was crazy how easy we all fit together so perfectly.

"I do feel the same," I answered finally. It wasn't a love proclamation, but he hadn't exactly done that either. I just hoped it was enough.

It must have been because the next thing I knew, my mouth was covered by his. Jack's hands cupped my backside, pressing me hard against his hardened length. Moaning into his mouth, I arched my back as I ground against him. For all my excuses, I wanted this more than I could ever really admit.

The others were more than happy to jump into the sack with me, feelings be damned. I had no idea how Raiden felt about me and knew too well how Firestar felt.

Jack was a different creature altogether. A complicated enigma I found myself wanting to unravel at every opportunity. Finally, I might have my chance.

My hands found their way into Jack's open shirt the coolness of his skin greeted my touch. How he could be so cold to the touch when from the way I was sweating it had to be over ninety degrees. I chalked it up to being part of his heritage and then wondered how he would feel inside of me. When I had him in my mouth, he'd hadn't warmed up any, even with my hot breath on him.

"What are you thinking about?" Jack pulled away from our kiss to ask.

I flushed and stared down at his chest, my fingers playing with the hair there. "About how you'd feel inside of me."

"Are you afraid?" he asked, his hand caressing my face once more concern on his own.

"No, no," I quickly assured him, shaking my head. "It's not that. More curious about the differences. I've only ever been with Raiden and Firestar, and they aren't quite as..." I trailed off as I looked for the right word. "Blessed."

Jack smiled a pleased sort of grin. "That is good to know, but you shouldn't fear. I wouldn't hurt you. We'll go slow. I know I am larger than others."

A sudden thought came to mind, and before I

could stop myself I blurted out, "Have you been with many women?"

His eyes widened at my question, clearly startled by my outburst. "Not as many as you would think and none that mattered."

My heart swelled at his words, loving how he dismissed his past lovers so easily, but also hoping he never did the same to me. To distract myself from the overwhelming amount of emotion inside of me, I cupped his face and pressed up on to my toes to claim his lips once more.

Tongues tangled together, I nipped and sucked at his lips until I needed to pull back to breathe. I dragged his shirt off his shoulders and found the buttons of his pants. Before I could undo them, Jack stopped me. His eyes bore into me as his own hands found the bottom of my top. I lifted my hands above my head and let him drag my shirt over my head.

The heat of the sun pressed down on my skin as I reached back and unsnapped my bra. My nipples were hard despite the warmth and when they brushed against Jack's chest, I let out a shiver. Jack's hand cupped my breasts, and then he knelt on the ground. His mouth was nothing like his skin, hot and wet, it covered the tip of my breast. My hands found his hair as his teeth skimmed my nipple pulling a groan from my throat.

He tortured me until I felt like I was on the verge of exploding. I tugged at his hair, forcing him to stand up and release my breast. My breathing heavy, I answered the unspoken question in his eyes. "We don't have time."

Gritting his teeth, Jack grabbed hold of my pants and pulled them down in one swift movement. I stepped out of them as I helped him remove his own. Arms wrapped around his neck, we lowered down to the ground together. My mouth found his as I straddled his lap, his hard, thick length pressed between us.

I rubbed myself against him, jolts of hot need shooting from between my thighs. My wet folds covered him, sliding along his length and making us both moan together. Jack's fingers slid against me, dipping inside and then out while I bucked against his hand, desperate for more. Grabbing him, I tried to line him up, but he shook his head.

"Not yet."

"Oh, come on," I cried out, my patience breaking. "You can't be backing out now. Not when we are so close."

Jack chuckled and pressed his lips to mine in a

short but sweet kiss. "I have no intentions of stopping, but if we don't prepare you, it will hurt quite a bit. And as I said, I never intend to hurt you, ever."

Frowning at his words, I tried to process what he said but came up blank. "How are you going to pre–?"

I choked on the words as Jack's fingers slid inside of me. Swallowing, I held onto his shoulders tightly. He moved his hand rubbing every inch of me inside and out. When he added another finger, I cried out. If I thought being with Raiden and Jack had felt like an unusual amount of fullness, right now I felt as if I were about to break in two. A burning need settled inside of me, and I couldn't make myself move.

"Hush now," Jack murmured, "It'll get better, I promise." His other hand came around to caress my bundle of nerves as he slowly began to move again. I hissed out, my eyes closing tight but eventually as he said the burning feeling dissipated and all that was left in its place was a hot need.

Both hands on his shoulders, I lowered myself, repeatedly riding his hand like I wanted to do to him. I gasped and screamed as he crooked his fingers inside and then seconds later stars exploded behind my eyes.

While I was coming down from my high, Jack quickly removed his fingers and lined us up, but before he could press into me voices came from the trees.

"Fuck," I growled my eyes going to where Raiden and Firestar had gone. "They can't be back already." I turned my attention back to Jack and grabbed his face in my hands. "Quickly before they get here." I rubbed myself on the head of him urging him to put it in.

"I'm telling you," Raiden's voice could be clearly made out now. "That meat had to be rotten, I've never had the shits like that in my entire life. I felt like my whole ass was about to fall out."

"You are disgusting," Firestar replied as they seemed to make sure to crack every branch as they made their way back.

"I am sorry, my love." Jack brushed my hair away from my face. "Maybe another time." Then he removed me from his lap and stood. His hard-on standing proudly as he pulled his pants back on.

I didn't move from the ground even as he held out his hand to me. I shook my head and wrapped my arms around my legs. I didn't care about my nakedness or that they guys would see me and know we hadn't done it. Only about how we had been so close and once again we had stopped. Sure, I'd gotten off, but it wasn't the same.

Tears pricked my eyes, and I cursed at myself for being so sensitive. This had nothing to do with Jack or me. Neither of us had stopped because we wanted to. Fate was an ugly bitch, and I was tired of her interference.

"Hey," Raiden said as he entered the camp. His eyes found me sitting on the ground a frown covering his face. When they found Jack's brooding face, he threw his hands up and cried out, "Really? You still didn't do it?"

"No," Jack snapped and turned away, heading toward the bags. When Jack didn't embellish on it, his gaze turned back to me, but I could only shrug, not trusting myself to answer.

"Well, maybe when we get to Raiden's home," Firestar knelt beside me and offered me my clothes. I took them but didn't feel like putting them on. My heart and body ached both for two different reasons.

Dammit.

7

The sky was dark when we finally arrived in the Eastern lands. Thunder crackled, and lightning lit the sky though there was no rain. Large expansions of rolling hills covered the area, reminding me of my own home in the Western lands.

"Beautiful, isn't it?" Raiden asked as we landed on a nearby hill. It had been Jack's turn to carry me, but I had asked Raiden to do it instead. I'd gotten plenty of questioning looks from that request, but I didn't answer any of them.

I knew it wasn't Jack's fault we had to stop, but I still felt hurt all the same. Out of the three of them, Jack seemed to have the strongest hold on my heart. Which seemed strange to me since Firestar and I had so much history, but then again, our relationship had started when I was not much more than a child. How could I know if what I had felt then was really love? Or if it even was now.

"It's wonderful," I answered as I tied my hair back. The wind had picked up the moment we had entered Raiden's lands, and it was doing its best to whack me in the face with my hair at every opportunity.

"Is it always like this?" I asked, nodding to the lit-up sky.

"No, not really," Raiden answered with a shrug. "We usually get lots of rain. While there is a long period every year where we don't have any, sadly this isn't one of them." He turned to Firestar with a teasing grin and smacked him on the back. "I wouldn't train in the yard if I were you. You'll fizzle out."

Firestar shrugged him off with a glare. "I'll be fine."

"What about you?" Raiden turned to Jack. "Any chances you'll melt from all the rain? Though, I suppose you can't get any watery than you have been the last day or so."

Jack ignored Raiden and rightly so, but his words caused me to frown. The tension in our group had risen since Jack and I's last failed attempt to consummate our relationship. Either because both of us felt like it was fate tearing us apart or because we were angry at the guys for interrupting us. Then again, I didn't know what the hell Jack was thinking most of the time. For all I knew, he was mad at me for being so upset.

I winced as I shifted in place. I could still feel Jack where he had stretched me not a day ago. If just his fingers could cause such an ache, I couldn't imagine how it would be when we finally got together completely. I might not even be able to walk.

The thought made my lips curl up into a grin. If I was too sore, I could always demand the ice dragon kiss it until I felt better, he had quite a way with his tongue. A new kind of ache filled my core, and a chorus of growls answered in return.

I turned to find three pairs of eyes watching me. I shrugged. "What? I can't help my body gets turned on at odd thoughts."

"What were you thinking about, Maya?" Firestar asked, taking a step toward me. "Maybe we could make a detour before heading to the palace."

Raiden and Firestar prowled toward me, licking their lips like I was some tasty meal they couldn't wait to devour. Jack, on the other hand, stood back, though there was longing in his eyes. It was that look that made me put my hands up.

"Stop, not here. We will have plenty of time to play when we get to Raiden's home." My eyes searched the area for danger. "Who knows who could be watching, waiting for us to let our guard down?" I glanced at Raiden. "You did say your brothers were warring, right?"

Raiden's expression sobered, and he stopped trying to come closer. "Yes, you are right. We shouldn't let our guard down until we know exactly what is going on. Come." He waved a hand for us to follow. "Let's get inside before the sky breaks."

We followed Raiden over the hill and down into a plain. The grass blew from the high gusts of wind as we rose to the top of the next hill. On the other side, sat a large stone fortress. Calling it a castle would have been too nice.

The walls were tall, so tall the hill couldn't even look over them. The towers on each corner were not decorative and stood short and thick as if to withstand the highest of winds. The fortress sat a bit higher than the town below which was surrounded by an even thicker wall of stone.

"Wow," I commented after a moment. "Are you expecting lots of invaders?"

Raiden shrugged. "When you live in a place like lightning valley, it's best to be prepared for anything. You won't find any grass or wooden homes here. Everything is hard as stone to withstand that." He pointed up at the sky which had darkened just in the short time we had landed.

Hurrying behind Raiden to the entrance of the stone structure, I couldn't help but be in awe of its magnitude. Even if it was specifically built to withstand the weather, I didn't imagine anyone wanting to try to climb those walls. They were slick from the previous rains no doubt and any foothold would slide right off. Of course, most dragons would have flown right over it, but I imagined they had ways to stop such attacks.

"Who goes there?" a voice called out from atop of the stone entrance.

"Raiden, youngest son of your lord and master. I have returned home to answer my father's pleas for assistance. Please let us pass before the sky opens up on our heads." Raiden hollered up to the mysterious voice.

After a moment, a head peeked out. I couldn't make any details out but a dark head of hair. They seemed to look over our party and then countered with, "And who have you brought with you? Foreigners?"

Raiden sighed and stomped his feet, muttering under his breath about idiot guards before he replied, "These are my friends and no business of yours."

"I'm sorry, Prince Raiden, but we cannot let you pass with unknown guests." The guard was starting to irritate me.

"Then get my father because I'm not going to explain myself to you," Raiden snarled up at the guard. "And when he comes and tells you to let us pass, you better hope it is before we all get drenched, or I'll beat the living daylights out of you."

The guard didn't reply, but his head jerked out of the window. Hopefully, he was getting Raiden's father and not leaving us there. I'd hate for us to have to fly over the gate. That definitely wouldn't make a very good impression on his family.

Firestar snorted at Raiden's threat and shook his head. Clearly, he wasn't impressed by the lightning dragon's threats. I wouldn't doubt for a second Firestar's would have been more graphic and bloody.

Jack, on the other hand, stood as quiet as ever, his hands behind his back as if he had all day to wait. Which he did, but they didn't know that. For all they knew, he could be planning their demise, he had that kind of blank expression.

I couldn't care less about some no-name guard, but if it would get us inside before we got soaked to the bone, I was all for threats. In most cases, it was the only way to get anyone to do what you wanted. My father had taught me that.

We waited for at least twenty minutes. The sky kept getting darker, and the thunder and lightning kept growing louder. Then, just as I felt a drop on my face, the stone doors creaked open.

Shifting into a fighting stance, we waited to see if the doors revealed a friend or foe. Raiden had said they were in a civil war. Maybe his brothers didn't want us there interfering, and this was their way of telling us to get lost.

"Father!" Raiden cried as soon as the doors opened completely.

Lord Shen was the spitting image of Raiden, or rather Raiden was the spitting image of his father. With olive skin and black hair, the sharp line of his nose was a dead ringer for his son. They even had the same goofy grin. A part of me found it weird that they looked so alike because while I was attracted to Raiden, I wasn't particularly attracted to Raiden's father. Probably because I'd fallen for Raiden's personality as much as his looks.

"Raiden, my boy!" Lord Shen opened his arms to his son, engulfing him in a hug. Standing side by side like that, it was hard to tell who was the father and who was the son, especially since they both favored opened-necked shirts. For a man with three grown children, Lord Shen had not let his body go soft. He was as hard and muscled as any of the men with me, and I had no doubt he could fight just as well.

"It's good to see you," Raiden said after a moment. "You need better guards."

Lord Shen frowned and shook his head. "I'm sorry about all that, but it is necessary for these troubling times."

Raiden's brow furrowed. "Surely my brothers are not feuding so much to need to question every person who comes to visit?"

His father sighed and rubbed his face, his eyes showing his age. "Not your brothers, the raiders."

"Raiders?" I asked, stepping forward. "Raiden mentioned you had some raids, but I didn't expect them to be that bad. Just some run of the mill thieves."

"If only they were, my dear," Raiden's father answered. "But sadly, that is not the case. They don't discriminate, they attack the rich and the poor. Sometimes not even stealing anything. It is as though they wish only to cause destruction. It is disheartening not to know what your enemies want. It makes it harder to get rid of them."

"You could just kill them all and be done with it," Firestar interjected, making me frown. Of course, that was his first thought in solving any problem.

Lord Shen didn't reply to Firestar's suggestion. Instead, he shook his head once more and smiled, "Where are my manners, all this talk of war and sadness and I don't know who any of you are."

Before I could introduce myself, Lord Shen came over to me with a kind smile. "You, my dear, must be Maya."

I smiled in return and nodded my head. Without warning, he pulled me into his embrace. "Hugs for family, my dear, and from what I hear, you very well may be family soon."

The thought of being part of Raiden's family made my heart warm. It couldn't be any worse than my own. I'd have loved for a happy welcome from my father without all the domineering drama. But I was a bit short on wishing stars at the moment.

Patting Lord Shen on the back awkwardly, I let him hug me for a moment before he finally pulled back but didn't let me go. His dark eyes, the same shade as Raiden's looked over me and then settled on my stomach, and I knew what he would say next.

"And what's this I hear about a grandchild?" Lord Shen glanced back at his son and then to me. "I never thought I'd be a grandfather before I died what with the way my sons seem to be determined to stay bachelors. I know your mother is very happy to hear of it."

I bit my tongue to keep myself from telling him the truth as guilt ate at me. He seemed like a nice enough man, and I didn't want to lie to him too. I'd left home so we wouldn't have to continue the lie, but it seemed like the news had spread far and wide. Just what I didn't need.

"It could very well be one of the others, father," Raiden reminded him with a nod to Jack and Firestar. "We have all decided to take Maya as our mate. We won't know whose child it is until it is born."

I waited for his father to explode like mine had, but Lord Shen threw his head back and laughed. "Ah, so not only do I have a new daughter-in-law but two more sons as well." He approached Firestar and clapped him on the back before he did the same with Jack. "Hopefully, you two can keep my youngest child in line. He's been known to get a bit out of control at times, but then again, he gets it from his father."

"You aren't upset?" I asked with a raised brow. Maybe I had been quick to judge the older dragon. Not everyone would have the same opinion as my father. At least I hoped not.

"Of course not!" Lord Shen announced. "You are young and fertile. I say spread the seed around. We need more babies in this world of all kinds. What better way to ensure our lines go on then to take every chance you can? Doesn't hurt that you have three strapping men to help make the process fun, either?" Lord Shen winked at me, making my face heat.

"And you," Lord Shen addressed the men. "You should be thankful you have such a lovely woman for your mate. It could be a lot worse. My first wife, god rest her soul, was a nice enough woman, but so commonly I had to get prepped beforehand."

"Father!" Raiden chastised but laughed all the same. Oh, to have such a relationship with one's father. Plenty of people would kill for it. I knew I would.

"Very well," Lord Shen sighed but grinned all the same. "Let's go inside, shall we? There is much to do and none of its getting done out here."

We followed Lord Shen past the wall and what I could only assume was the guard who had stopped us. His eyes widened as we passed, and the scent of fear filled my nose. Raiden's threat had not been for nothing. Just as we entered the fortress completely, the skies opened, and rain poured down on top of us, completely soaking us through.

Just great.

8

Following behind Lord Shen, we walked along the streets of the capital city. There were several peculiarities I noticed straight away. Ones that caused my suspicion to rise.

If my father had walked through the city - which he rarely ever did - he'd have at least a dozen guards with him. Not that our city was particularly dangerous, but he didn't want to give anyone a chance to stab him in the back.

"Fickle creatures," he'd call them before continuing on, "They love you one day but would have no qualms about killing you the next."

Lord Shen did not seem to have any of those concerns. He strolled down the street as if he were completely at ease. He had a total of one guard -

one - and while he was large and menacing, he stayed a few feet behind our party. If there were any trouble, he wouldn't do any good there.

But Lord Shen's lack of protection wasn't even the strangest part of it all. Not by far. In the midst of a civil war, I expected to find fear and empty streets through the kingdom. Maybe even damage from past fighting.

None of those things were present. In fact, the streets were packed with stalls. Vendors called out to try their wares. Children played while their parents gossiped a watchful eye on them the entire time. No one would look at this city and think there was anything other than peace within its walls.

"Lord Shen," Jack said, his eyes scanning the area as well. "I do not mean to be intrusive, but didn't you say that your sons were feuding?"

"Ah yes," Lord Shen nodded his head. "Quite so. Terrible thing it is too. The number of key limes I've had to buy has been absolutely ridiculous."

Jack and I exchanged a confused look. Key limes? What did that have to do with anything?

Instead of Lord Shen filling in the blanks, Raiden answered for him. "My brothers are not the normal sort of princes. They have their own way of sorting out their differences."

"And those require fruit?" I cocked a brow at him.

Raiden shrugged. "Better than starting a war."

"So, why does it look like the people don't even know anything about it?" I gestured around us to the happy going people of the Eastern lands. Not even back on Earth had people looked so at ease.

"Oh, they know," Lord Shen answered. "They take great pride in betting on the outcome." He cleared his throat and adjusted his shirt before adding, "I, myself, have placed a bet or two these last few weeks."

"Father!" Raiden looked at him with surprise on his face. "That's hardly fair."

"I don't always bet on one of them, sometimes it's both," Lord Shen explained. "Besides, it's good for the morale and the economy. If I lose, the people get a large sum of money from the Lord of the North himself."

It did make sense. Definitely, a selfless thing to do as the ruler of the land. My father would never have done such a thing, not unless he profited from it. I was beginning to see why Raiden cared for his father so much.

"But what exactly are you betting on?" Firestar asked, stroking his chin as if deep in thought.

"Who will win the next attack, of course?" Lord Shen shook his head like it was easily deduced.

I caught up to Lord Shen's side and placed my hand on his arm. "I apologize, my lord, but you have to understand our confusion. To us, a civil war includes bloodshed and mayhem. Pillaging and destruction." I swept a hand around the busy street. "None of those things are found here. How are your sons fighting it out if none of the people are involved?"

Lord Shen placed his hand on top of mine and laughed. "Oh, my dear. Not all fights have to be on the battlefield. Some are best kept in the family." That was all he said about it before we came to the end of the main part of the town and to the doors of the palace.

A loud roar filled the sky, and everyone on the ground looked up. Two dragons the size of houses soared above us, long and windy like snakes, they slithered through the sky. Each of their scales was as bright and yellow as the sun and from what I could tell on the ground, identical.

The dragons roared and hissed, one shooting fire at the other only to miss. The other dragon spun around in the air, swiping his tail at his opponent. His attack didn't miss, but it hardly seemed to affect the other dragon at all. In fact, if I didn't know any better, I would think he was laughing at his counterpart.

"What the hell do they think they are doing?" Raiden asked his hands on his hips as he shook his head. "No dragon in his right mind would fight above the city. They're going to break something."

"Their heads more than likely," his father commented. "They do this every day now. Mostly posturing, they never really try to hurt the other. You'd think the pranks would be enough, but no, they need to put on a show for everyone. Shameful really."

I eyed the dragons above us for another moment before it clicked. My head jerked to look at Lord Shen and Raiden my mouth open wide. "Wait a minute, are you telling me those dragons…" I pointed up at the battling dragons. "Are your brothers?"

Raiden nodded before crossing his arms over his chest and pursing his lips together in a grimace. "Unfortunately. You'd think as the older ones they would have more sense in their heads, but it seems all intelligence has flown away with my leaving."

"That it has, my boy." Lord Shen laughed and clapped his son on the back. "Hopefully, you can talk some sense into those two. You've always been the most level-headed of the three of my children."

"Raiden? Level headed?" Firestar snorted, earning him a warning glare from Raiden. "If they are worse than you, I'm not sure I want to meet them."

"I concur," Jack said with a nod. "One careless dragon is enough."

"Hey!" Raiden shouted, but when the two of them laughed, he joined in.

For all our problems, I was happy they were getting along so well. It could have been worse. They could hate each other. Or they could bicker all the time, and I would get stuck in the middle acting as mediator. Just thinking about it gave me a headache. I counted my blessing that at least I didn't have to worry about that.

Now, if only I could get pregnant.

Nevertheless, I had to agree with Firestar and Jack. One Raiden was enough. I couldn't imagine how his brothers really were. My own brother had died before I had turned twelve. I'd hardly gotten to know him before he had been taken away from us.

The problem with wars was people died, and usually, it was the ones you loved and not those who deserved it. Maybe Raiden's brothers had it right.

No need to involve the people, work it out between themselves and leave the rest out of it. Surely there were fewer casualties that way?

"You've got your thinking face on," Raiden said as he took my arm in his. He let the rest of our party go ahead through the palace halls. I had been too deep in thought to really pay much attention to them, but they weren't anything out of the ordinary. Not barren like Firestar's home or extravagant like my father's. Overall, I'd have to say they reflected their lords very well.

Strong and sturdy to protect their people but massive enough that it had to be a constant joke between them. I could just hear the laughter as they poked at each other about overcompensating for something else.

"Tell me about your brothers," I said after a moment. "What are they like? Are they as your father said? Like you?"

"Well," Raiden started scratching the back of his head. "They are like me but not. They're some of the greatest warriors I know but prefer to pull pranks than to actually fight. You'll have to see them to understand."

Chewing on my bottom lip, I grew concerned. I didn't particularly like surprises. I wanted to know what I was going up against rather than wait and see. But Raiden and his father seemed hell-bent on letting me make up my own mind. Which was a bad idea, if I did say so myself.

We walked up a staircase, which opened into a large room. In the room lay a stone table with a handmade map of all Waesigar. I'd have loved to study it at length, but there were more interesting things, and the brothers had just transformed back into human form.

Raiden hadn't been kidding when he said his brothers were like him and his father. What he hadn't mentioned was the fact that they were twins. One of the brothers had short hair with shaved sides decorated with a lightning bolt along each side.

The other one also had shaved hair but only on one side. The other side was kept long and hanging down to his chest. That was where the differences ended. Besides their hair and clothes, they were exactly the same. Piercing dark eyes and full lips that I had no doubt resulted in dimples when they smiled. They weren't smiling now though.

"You don't know what you are talking about, little brother," the one with long hair growled. "We will be slaughtered in our sleep going that route."

"And what about you, big brother?" the short haired one sneered. "Are we to just destroy them without finding out where they came from? Why they are here? For all you know, more will just come to replace them."

Lord Shen cleared his throat, placing his hands behind his back as he waited for the bickering brothers to notice us. It didn't take long. The clearing of their father's voice made them look our way, their words dying in their throat.

"Raiden!" they shouted in unison and charged toward us. Jack grabbed hold of me and shoved me backward before I could get trampled. The three brothers were completely unaware of the rest of us as they talked all at once, smacking each other on the back and laughing.

"Where have you been?" the long-haired brother asked.

"We thought you were too busy knocking that western princess up to come visit us?" the short-haired one teased.

At the mention of me, the Western princess, Raiden's face sobered. He found me with his eyes and cleared his throat, moving away from his brothers. Rubbing the back of his head, his ears turned pink. Was Raiden embarrassed? The very thought made me smile and want to tease him the way he always messed with me.

His brothers noticed the change in him and followed his gaze. When it landed on me, their grins widened and then it was I who was being smashed between them. Jack and Firestar started forward as if to remove them, but I held a hand up. I wasn't against a bit of hugging if that was all that it was.

"So, you're the beauty who has our little brother all in knots?" one brother asked before adding, "I'm Fujin by the way."

The short-haired brother then said, "And I'm Raijin. Feel free to mix them up, everyone does."

"Wait, I thought your names were Aido and Dred?" I tossed a glance at Raiden who smiled.

"You told her our real names?" Raijin exclaimed, narrowing his eyes at Raiden. "How could you?"

"Wait, what?" I asked, suddenly confused.

"Those are our names, sure, but not our better names," Fujin said with a shrug, and I couldn't help but smile at them as they both glared at their younger brother.

"I'm not quite following," I said, glancing at Raiden for an explanation, but before he could say anything, Raijin jumped in.

"Those are the names the man gave us to keep us down, but we prefer our new names." Raijin smirked, his eyes settling on me. "And don't you dare say otherwise."

"I don't think that will be a problem." I giggled as they released me but didn't move away.

"Good, I'd hate for it to be one." Raijin stuck out his tongue at me before shifting his eyes to his father. "Honestly, who names a son Dreq?"

Before their father could respond, Fujin settled his eyes on me, gripping my hands tightly and giving me an excited shake before turning to Raiden.

"You brother, are a liar," Fujin said with a wag of his finger. "You wrote that about her loveliness, but when we asked about her ability to produce heirs, you were all closed lips. We concluded she had to be a fragile little thing." He gestured toward me with a wicked grin. "But I don't see any weakness in her. She looks like she could take whatever you put out."

"Hey!" Raiden stepped in pushing his brothers back. "You don't get to talk about her that way, and besides, she's not just mine."

The brothers glanced at Firestar and Jack before they tried to engulf them in hugs as well. Firestar apparently had had enough hugs for one day and produced a fireball in his hand, holding it in front of him in a silent threat. Jack too did not want to be hugged, but he simply stepped away with a shake of his head and offered them a half bow. So, surprised by his actions the brothers couldn't do anything but bow in return.

"This is Firestar and Jack," Raiden said after they finished trying to embrace them. "They too are Maya's suitors."

"And you are okay with this?" Fujin asked, raising a brow.

Raiden shrugged. "They're good men and even better dragons, I don't see why I wouldn't be."

Raijin launched himself at Raiden, putting the younger brother in a headlock. "Yeah, Fujin, our little brother had to learn to share more than us. He's used to getting sloppy seconds."

"Now, wait just a minute," I growled, anger filling me. "I'm no one's sloppy seconds. I care for Raiden as much as the others. I don't rate any of them lower than the others, and I don't appreciate you insinuating such."

"Our apologies," Fujin bowed to me with a small smile. "We meant no harm. Only brothers giving each other crap."

"Yeah," Raiden agreed, having gotten loose of Raijin. "They are just messing around, and besides, I'm used to it."

"Doesn't make it right," I pointed out, crossing my arms over my chest with a stern frown.

"You're right it doesn't." Raiden nodded and then smirked. "Besides, I wasn't second, I was first."

His brothers burst out laughing along with Raiden. Even his father chuckled a bit. Jack and Firestar didn't on the other hand. They didn't seem to like the joke any more than I did.

Thankfully, Jack changed the subject before we really got into it. "Your father was telling us about your disagreement?"

"Ah, yeah." Fujin rubbed his chin. "The disagreement."

"Yeah," Raiden frowned turning to his brothers. "Father said you were practically tearing yourselves apart, and he feared a civil war."

Fujin and Raijin rolled their eyes in unison, and then Raijin said, "Father exaggerates. We simply have a different opinion on how to handle raiders and have yet to come to a decision."

"And while you are bickering up here in the palace, putting on your shows and playing your pranks, the people outside the city are suffering,"

Lord Shen interjected with a sober expression. "You need to decide what to do and do it soon, or there may not be any of our lands left to inherit."

"We know," both brothers said at once.

"What's the problem exactly?" I asked finally. All this beating around the bush nonsense was getting tiresome.

"Well, this idiot thinks we should talk to the raiders." Fujin pointed a thumb at Raijin. "While I think we should kill them all."

"It would be more proactive to send a message," Firestar said, placing his hands on the table where the map sat. "If you drew them to one of the smaller villages and gave the citizens an evacuation order. You could get the jump on them before they can do any more damage."

"That's a good idea," Fujin agreed, looking at the map with Firestar. "But bonehead here will never agree to it."

"You got that right," Raijin shot back and then turned to the rest of us. "Now, enough talk of raids and such. Our baby brother has returned, and with his lady love, that's cause for celebration!"

Raiden laughed along with his brother. "You just want an excuse to get drunk."

"So," Raijin shrugged. "You would too with this guy as your other half."

His words only made his twin launch into a long-winded speech about how he had gotten all the intelligence in the womb and Raijin had none. I tuned them out not more than five minutes into it.

"He wasn't kidding, was he?"

I looked up at Jack who stood by my side. "About what?"

"They are exactly the same."

"Oh," I giggled and leaned into his side. "It would seem so"

"Yes, it is. I just hope the brothers' bickering will not cause issues for us," Jack mused, and I had to agree. We were supposed to be here to get away from complications, but I had a feeling Raiden's brothers were going to be an even bigger complication all on their own.

9

They had offered us one room for all four of us, but we had quickly declined. While the men had no qualms about sharing me, we were all happy to have our own area. Room to breathe as it were.

"Do you want something else to wear?" Raiden asked as he helped me unpack the few items we had brought. Jack and Firestar had gone to their rooms to clean up or whatnot. Only Raiden had stayed behind.

"No." I shook my head and smiled. I hadn't expected there to be a party, so I hadn't packed for one. A dress would have been more appropriate for the party, but I couldn't bring myself to wear one.

Here I didn't have to pretend to be pregnant, so loose clothing wasn't required. I'd savor that freedom as long as I could.

"Are you sure?" Raiden fingered my shirt. "Aren't you tired of wearing these dusty clothes?"

Raising a brow, I sat on the edge of the bed my arms over my chest. "What if I want to wear my dusty clothes?"

"Then that is your right." Raiden shrugged and then stood before me his hands on either side of my hips. "But I would think you would like to clean up. We will be meeting quite a few people tonight. Including my mother."

I cocked my head to the side and smirked. "Are you worried your mother won't like me?"

"No, no," Raiden quickly said and then paused before saying, "My mother hates everyone."

We exchanged a look for a moment before laughing. It seemed like we both had bothersome family members. Firestar and I both had irksome fathers, of course, it would be only natural that Raiden with his fun-loving attitude would need a reason for one. A nasty mother would fit right in.

"So," I said after we had finished laughing. "If your mother won't like me, why does it matter what I wear?"

"Because." Raiden pressed his forehead against mine. "You will only give her more ammo to use against you. I already know she will hate the fact that I agreed to share you, I don't want you to get hurt."

"Hurt?" I asked, placing my hands on his arms as I leaned into his embrace. "Have you forgotten who my father is? Do you think his horrible words are a new occurrence? I've been spoken down to all my life, if I don't have thick enough skin to handle it by now, I would be a sad dragon indeed."

Raiden didn't say anything after that, but I could tell he was still worried. I dragged my hands through his hair ruffling it for good measure before I sighed. "I suppose I could take a shower and maybe even put on a clean pair of clothes but," I held a finger up. "I'm not wearing a dress."

"I can respect that." Raiden chuckled and slid his hands onto my hips, shifting himself between them. "Though, I know quite a few ways a dress would be a blessing." He rubbed himself against my center, making me gasp. "Like in this instance, if you were wearing a dress now," he murmured as he lifted my legs to wrap around his waist. "I could easily slide into you now, but since you aren't, I have to go to all the trouble of disrobing you." His mouth brushed against mine, licking my lips but never finishing the kiss.

"What's stopping you?" I whispered though I didn't know why. We were alone, and no one would hear me. Not that I cared if they did.

Raiden smiled against my lips. "Nothing," he admitted before ripping my shirt off my body. My own hands pulled at the opening of his shirt until it hung off him in shreds. Before I could get my hands on his pants, he shoved me back on the bed. I lifted my hips as he dragged my pants off my legs and threw them to the floor.

Unsnapping his pants, he released himself and then without warning plunged himself inside of me. I let out a choking gasp as I clutched the bed beneath me. Not as prepared as usual, the fit was tighter than I remembered and a slight burning filled low inside of me.

Hips thrusting against me, Raiden pulled me back up from the bed until our mouths met. Tongues and teeth fighting, I wrapped my legs tightly around his waist and my hands digging into his scalp as I rode him. Raiden dipped his hand between us and circled my sensitive nub, and I cried out as my pleasure swelled.

I tried to move us faster, to keep the momentum going, but I didn't have the leverage. Raiden seemed to notice and shifted us so he sat on the edge of the bed. With my knees firmly planted on the bed, I rose up and slammed back down on him. Raiden groaned, and I hissed as he hit deep inside of me.

We moved together with my front rubbing against him, shooting bolts of lightning through my nerves. Hands on my hips, Raiden helped me move on top of him our eyes locking together. This man had come into my life not long ago. Took me to his bed and into his heart. Not unlike the others, but he had also touched a part of me the others didn't.

He made me laugh. Many a woman would agree that a man who could make you laugh was worth more than all the riches in the world. That and a solid orgasm or two.

My lips ticked up at the thought just as my release caught up with me. Throwing my head back, I screamed, my nails digging into Raiden's shoulders as I came. Too distracted by the pleasure, Raiden took over our movement. Before I could come down from my high, I was hit with it again, but this time Raiden cried out with me.

Breathing heavily, I pressed my face to the top of Raiden's head. His lips pressed against my chest, right where my heart sat, and I couldn't have loved him more in that instant.

A funny thing it was, love. I had three men courting me. Three who had my bed - or mostly – and all three of them made my heart swell with joy just from seeing them.

"What now?" I asked, pulling back from him.

Raiden chuckled and swiped a bead of sweat from my neck. "Now, it's time for a bath." His eyes glanced out the window at the setting sun. "Or rather a very quick shower."

I screeched as he lifted us from the bed and toward the bathroom. While we had all intentions of bathing quickly, it didn't quite happen that way. Water and soap made things slippery which in turn tempted our hands to do more than washing.

Hand between my thighs, Raiden played me to my release until my knees buckled beneath me. Then when with me bent over at the waist, he took me again from behind, our skin slapping in the spray of the water until the liquid went cold.

We stumbled from the shower shivering and laughing. To not be tempted and even more delayed we dried ourselves off, though our eyes kept finding each other. My cheeks had begun to hurt from smiling so much, and I couldn't remember the last time I had been so happy. I imagined it probably had been back on Earth where no one wanted anything from me.

As we finished drying off, I asked Raiden, "You said your mother is a difficult woman. Do we have any reason to fear her or your family with our ... secret?"

Raiden seemed to think about it for a moment before he said no longer smiling, "She's my mother."

"That doesn't answer anything," I accused. "Dannan is my father, but do you think I would trust him with this secret? He'd have me lined up to be taken by every man in his guard just so he could increase his power base. Can you say the same about yours?"

"Oh. That secret." He shook his head in denial. "No, no. She wouldn't betray me that way, nor would my father or brothers. They are trustworthy. You have nothing to fear from them." He took my hands in his and pressed them to his lips. "I would never let anything happen to you."

His words were meant to be reassuring, and I forced a smile on my lips even as a sinking feeling took up residence in my stomach, and I tried to push it away but without hope. I didn't doubt Raiden's words. I was sure he believed every one of them. But the best of us knew that family could betray you worse than anyone else.

10
___

We were all ready for whatever the night held. Which if we were lucky would mean a short evening and a soft pillow soon after. But from the way Raiden carried on with his brothers, I highly doubted that would be possible.

"I'm telling you," Raiden stood by my bedroom door and smacked Firestar on the arm with a laugh. "You've never been to a party until you've partied with an easterner. There will be wine and dancing - and food! The food," he licked his lips, his eyes gleaming at the prospect, "is better than anything you have ever tasted in your life."

Firestar and I exchanged a look as Raiden went

on to describe all the types of food we'd encounter. I couldn't really think of food now. The occupancy of my stomach had increased the closer the party came. I had to have a whole flock of butterflies in there by now, all fluttering about making me want to stay curled up in my bed.

It didn't help that Jack had been quieter than usual. I didn't know what bug was up his butt, but I could guess it had something to do with us not being together completely. Unfortunately, his bad mood wasn't helping my stress level any.

"All right, all right," I interrupted Raiden who would keep us there all night describing what would happen rather than letting us go find out for ourselves. "Let's get going before all this glorious food has been gobbled up by your brothers."

"And they would!" Raiden cried out and then laughed. "The greedy bastards."

Raiden continued to poke fun at his brothers as he and Firestar left the room. I tried to follow him, but Jack caught my arm, stopping me.

"May I have a word?" Jack asked and then looked at the others. "We'll be on in a little bit."

Raiden and Firestar gave me a questioning look, but I only nodded for them to go. When they were gone, I turned back to Jack. "You wanted to speak to me."

Jack moved past me and closed the door. When we were in private, he stayed quiet. He paced back and forth for a moment as if he couldn't get his words together.

"Jack," I started, placing a hand on his arm to stop his pacing. "What's wrong?"

"I've been thinking."

I smiled slightly. "I can see that. You've been so quiet I was afraid you might turn into stone." When he didn't smile, I frowned. "Really, Jack. What has you all torn up?"

"I feel," Jack began but then stopped and sighed. "We're doing this all wrong."

"This?" I quirked a brow. "What's this?"

"Us." He adjusted his jacket and then folded his hands in front of him. "We keep thinking that for us to be together, we have to be together physically. But in all actuality, we don't."

Brow furrowed, I slowly asked, "We don't?"

"No."

When he didn't embellish on it, I tried to make sense of where he was going with his train of thought. "So, let me get this straight. You think that we are trying too hard to have sex which is why we can't have sex?"

"Correct."

"And then the fact that we need to sleep together, which will make it so I am no longer lying. You'd also actually have a chance at being the father, doesn't matter to you at all?" I scoffed not believing it for one second.

Jack's lips pressed together into a tight line. The ice dragon didn't like to be questioned? Well, too damned bad. His logic was stupid, and I wasn't going to let him talk me in circles.

"Why do we need your father's approval?" Jack asked after a moment. "How will he know if we lay together or not? I'm not going to tell him, are you?"

"Of course not." I shook my head in disgust. I wouldn't tell my father the time of day if he asked for it.

"And as far as whether I am the father," Jack continued before stepping closer to me and taking my hands. "I only want to be with you. Sure, I would love to have children with you one day, but it doesn't have to be the first or even the second child. I just want you."

"And I want to have children with you as well," I shook my head, smiling. "I could just imagine pretty little babies with white hair and your blue eyes. Nothing would make me happier. But you are forgetting one thing…"

"And what could that possibly be?" Jack tried to cut me off. I stared him down and then when he didn't catch on to my thoughts said, "If you and I don't have sex, you won't get the extra power boost like Firestar and Raiden—"

"I don't care about that."

"You might not," I countered, moving away from him and sitting on the edge of the bed. "But with all the attacks and now with Ned out for us too, we could use a bit of extra power. God knows I'm not contributing much to this foursome."

"That's not true," Jack argued, coming to sit beside me. "It's not like you are some helpless child. You can fight."

"Barely."

"And once you can fly, you will be a force to be reckoned with."

"If, you forgot if," I reminded him. "I'm no closer to being able to fly than when we first started this adventure if you can call it that." I rubbed my eyes already tired and ready to go to bed. Would the Lord and Lady of the East be offended if I begged off with the excuse of my fake child making me ill?

From the way Raiden talked about his mother, I highly doubted it.

"In any case," Jack interrupted my thoughts of sleep. "I think we should take a page out of Raiden and his family's book."

"And what's that?"

"That we should how do they say it," he paused for a moment before flicking his hair over his shoulder with a smirk. "Go with the flow."

"Go with the flow," I drew out and then huffed. "And what does that mean?"

Jack turned to me, putting one leg up on the edge of the bed. He cupped my face in his hands and leaned in close. "Do not stress about when our time will come. The more you want it, the harder it will be to have it."

I placed my hands on top of his, stroking his fingers. "So, we should just let it happen, is what you are saying?"

"Exactly." He pressed his lips to mine and then stood from the bed. Offering me a hand, he pulled me to my feet. "Now, let's go get rip-roaring drunk. I have a feeling that's the only way we're going to get through tonight."

I snorted as I followed him out of the room. "Unfortunately, I will have to suffer through the next few hours sober. I don't think Raiden's family would look too kindly on a pregnant woman drinking."

Jack squeezed my hand. "Then we best make the most of it."

We could hear the party before we saw it. The music played loudly, and the laughter was high. I hadn't heard such a commotion since I was back on Earth, celebrating the release of Waesigar, Land of the Dragons game.

The doors opened for us as we approached. The room was packed to the brim, barely leaving room for walking let alone dancing, but there was dancing nonetheless. Dancing like I'd never seen before. They moved like the dragons I had seen just earlier that day, slithering and writhing through the air. They moved together like a rehearsed dance, their bodies rubbing against each other in an almost provocative way.

"Would you like to dance?" Jack asked, leading me toward the dance floor.

Smiling like a fool, I let him pull me into his arms, but we only just began to move when Raiden approached with an older woman at his side. Hair as black as night, the white streaks through it only enhanced her beauty rather than lessen it. She had a modest build. Not like those lord's wives I'd seen before who had let themselves go after they'd had children. Lady Nariko seemed the type to be in control of everything, even what she ate.

Even if I couldn't figure out who she was, I would know she was not a woman to trifle with. There was a hardness in her eyes that came from a lifetime of experience. I'd imagine raising three men like Raiden would have to make anyone hard, especially with their father as her husband. Someone had to be the grown up.

And the Lady of the East definitely was.

"Maya Rose," Raiden said, bringing his mother forward. "May I present my mother, Lady Nariko. Mother, this is my mate, Maya." He then leaned in and muttered not too low. "Be nice."

Lady Nariko shot him a chastising look, the only way a mother could, before giving me a tight-lipped smile. "It is a pleasure to meet you, my dear."

"And you," I nodded to her, my hand on Jack's arm, which she noticed. By the pinching of her brows, and the press of her lips, I could tell she was not happy about it. Not one bit.

"I heard you have quite the harem on your hands," Lady Nariko glanced to at Jack before turning her gaze to where Firestar stood talking to

Raiden's brothers. "I don't know how you can handle so many men at once, I'd imagine it would get tiring. I barely have enough patience with the one I have."

I offered her a smile and a nervous chuckle. "It can be challenging at times." I exchanged a look with Raiden and Jack who smiled in return.

"Even more so now that you are pregnant." She raised a brow as if it were a question and not a statement. I had a feeling she didn't entirely believe I was pregnant. I'd found an amazing number of women were more suspicious than the men. Probably why we find ourselves with such difficult men because we could smell bullshit a mile away. Lady Nariko was no different. I'd have to be careful of her from now on.

"Yes," I answered, my own smile going thin. "It can be difficult. But you would know that having three sons all with strong personalities, I could imagine it would be quite a challenge to raise them and keep your sanity."

"Well, we do what we must," Lady Nariko paused and then added with a hint of warning, "We mothers tend to do whatever it takes to ensure the happiness and longevity of our children."

"I would expect nothing less. If you would

excuse me," I said, turning to Jack. "I'm feeling a bit tired, would you escort me back to the room?"

"Of course," Jack answered without question. He was smarter than the others. Firestar would have told me to let loose and quit worrying so much. Raiden, on the other hand, didn't question my request either but did raise a brow. At least, he had the wisdom not to voice those questions in front of his mother. It had been him that warned me about her.

"It was a pleasure to meet you." I nodded to Lady Nariko and allowed Jack to lead me away before she could say another word. I'd had enough backward threats and backhanded compliments in my lifetime. If I wanted more, I could go back home to my father.

Nevertheless, there was one thing I had learned from the encounter, Lady Nariko would not make this a pleasant visit, not at all. The way she looked at me like I was either an obstacle to overcome or something she could use, didn't bode well. I could only count the minutes until we left and yesterday could not be soon enough.

"Are you all right?" Jack asked once we were out of hearing distance.

"Yes," I answered as we walked down the

hallway and back to our rooms. "I just needed to get away from that vile woman."

"She seemed perfectly pleasant to me."

I snorted. "That's because you are a man. You don't see the subtleties in the way we women attack one another. Our conversation was the equivalent of knife fight in a locked closet."

"So, Lady Nariko doesn't like that you are with Raiden and all of us?" Jack raised a brow.

My arm was looped through his arm as we strolled through the hallway and back to our rooms.

"No," I said with a twisted grimace. "Not at all."

Lady Nariko's dislike for me was only one of the many problems she represented. Just a few minutes with her and I could tell what kind of woman she was. A cougar in a house full of kittens, she'd sooner eat her whole litter than let me have her baby boy. I'd met many like her before. But on Earth they were harder to deal with. I couldn't just beat the crap out of them. Couldn't do it to her either, but the idea had occurred to me. Not to forget how she hinted at knowing I wasn't pregnant. Why else would she keep asking so many questions about it?

We turned the corner down the hallway that

housed our bedrooms, but when we approached my door, Jack shoved me behind him. His hands began to glow the eerie white of his powers as he pressed a finger to his lips telling me to be quiet.

Not sure what was going on, I tried to see around him to my bedroom door which had been ripped open, so it barely hung by one metal hook. Jack pushed the door open further, causing it to fall to the ground with a loud thud. Jack and I tensed for an attack, but none came.

Flicking the lights on, Jack held up a hand for me to wait at the door. The room was trashed. My bed sheets had been torn to shreds. My small bag of clothes thrown all over the room. I'd have been upset about the ornate furniture so kindly provided by the Lord and Lady of the East, but now that I'd met Raiden's mother, I didn't feel so bad.

Nevertheless, whoever had come for me hadn't cared if they drew attention. If anything, they wanted people to know they were here. I'd been lucky not to be in the room at the time.

"Whoever they were," Jack said after he came out of the bathroom his hands no longer glowing. "They aren't here anymore."

I worried my bottom lip as I surveyed the damage. I knew I had plenty of enemies and was gaining more by the day it seemed but to so boldly attack me in the home of the Eastern Lord? They would have to be stupid or arrogant. I was betting on stupid.

"Come," Jack ushered me out of the destroyed room and across the hall to his room. "Stay in my room tonight, and we'll see about getting you a new room in the morning."

Sitting down on his bed, I placed my hands on my lap, forcing them not to shake. I'd been attacked before, but usually, it was out in the wilderness or on a training field. This person didn't want any witnesses. Why else attack in my room and not out in the open?

"Maya," Jack softly said, kneeling in front of me. He took my hands in his, a small comfort to my shaken nerves. "You are safe here. I won't let anything happen to you."

I nodded my head but didn't answer because my words were caught in my throat.

"I need to tell the others and Lord Shen. He will want to up his security if they were able to get this far without being caught." Jack stood and started for the door, but I held tight to his hand.

"Don't go." My words came out small and child-like even to me. Usually, I'd be berating myself for acting so cowardly, but at that moment, all I wanted was for someone to hold me to show me I was safe.

Jack came back to me, and I wrapped my arms around his middle, pressing my head to his stomach. Hands on my head, Jack stroked my hair until I hummed with pleasure. My fear started to ebb, and in its place, a deep seeded desire to have his skin pressed against mine grew.

Shifting my hold, I slid Jack's shirt up until I could press my mouth to his hard abdomen. Jack's stroking stopped, but I didn't. I unbuttoned his shirt from the bottom up, moving my mouth along him in a hot trail of open-mouthed kisses until I was kneeling on the bed. Now at eye level, I took Jack's face in my hands, covering his lips with my own.

We sat there for a moment just kissing before Jack eased me away. "Maya, are you sure about this? You're in shock. I wouldn't want to take—"

"Shut up and make love to me, Jack." I cut him off before covering his mouth with mine once more.

No more protests came from my ice dragon as I pushed his shirt and jacket off his shoulders and let them fall to the ground with a satisfying plop. Next, I wasted no time undoing his pants and giving them the exact same treatment. With Jack long and hard before me, I scrambled out of my own clothes, the need to press my heated skin against his too much for me to take.

Laying back on the bed, I guided Jack to me until he settled between my thighs. His long white hair skimmed my skin causing me to giggle slightly at the sensation. When Jack's eye snapped up to my face, I tried to sober my expression but couldn't and ended up laughing whole heartedly.

"You find me funny, woman," Jack growled against me, making my already aching center mew in pleasure.

"No." I shook my head violently but still smiled. "Your hair tickles."

"Oh." He raised a brow, and then his fingers found their way between my thighs, and I wasn't laughing more. "Does this tickle?"

"No," I gasped, arching my hips off the bed.

As his fingers thrust into me, his other hand found my most sensitive part. Stroking it until I cried out, he asked, "What about this?"

"Definitely not," I barely got out before my first orgasm hit me. My fingers tightened on the bed covers, and my hips bucked off the bed in wild succession. Jack grabbed something from behind me and shoved it underneath my hips as I came down.

A pillow. Why did he need a pillow?

The thought had barely come to my mind when Jack's tip pushed at my entrance. Achingly slow, Jack slid into me, making each inch count. Stretched as far as I could go, I had to force myself to remember to breathe. I knew Jack was bigger than the others, but the actual act of having him inside of me was something else completely.

"Are you all right?" Jack asked his voice strained. While I had a bit of discomfort from taking someone of his girth, he must be dying to move. Little beads of sweat slid down his face and dropped on to my stomach. For an ice dragon, I found the sight a bit funny, but I knew from previous experience now was not the time to mention it.

Instead, I licked my lips, wetting my dry mouth and nodded.

Without warning, Jack rocked his hips back in an agonizingly slow manner. He had almost completely removed himself from me, hitting every inch of the inside of me as he went and then in one quick movement pushed into me again. A choking gasp ripped through me as he hit the spot deep inside of me that made my toes curl.

I couldn't add much to the experience, my own body too overwhelmed by Jack's size. All I could do was hold on and enjoy the ride - which I did several times.

11

___

Sunlight poured through the windows of Jack's room. I stretched beneath the covers, a silly grin on my face. I hadn't felt so relaxed in my entire life. Who knew all I needed was someone like Jack to make all my worries disappear?

Speaking of which, I rolled over to see if Jack would be interested in some more fun but found the bed empty. I touched his side of the bed and found it cool. He'd been gone a while.

Irritation prickled at me as I stood from the bed. Instantly, I regretted it. A deep ache from between my thighs screamed at me as my legs tried to give out on me. I grabbed the side of the bed for balance and took a few deep breaths before trying to stand once more. Still hurt but better.

Wincing, I walked to the bathroom where I took the slowest shower known to man or dragon. Each movement made me gasp and wince, the memory of last night's activities coming to my mind. While being with Jack had indeed been an enjoyable experience, it had its consequences the next day.

As I climbed out of the shower, the bedroom door opened, and voices could be heard from the other room. I wrapped a towel around me before peeking my head out of the bathroom. All three of my suitors stood in Jack's room, and none of them looked happy.

"I thought you said she was here?" Firestar asked with a deepening frown.

"She was," Jack snapped back.

"Well, it doesn't look like it," Firestar argued with a wave of his hand. "How could you leave her alone? How do you know they didn't take her while you were gone?"

Instead of making my presence known, I leaned against the door frame of the bathroom and waited for them to notice me. From the way they were arguing, I doubted it would be soon.

"Now, hold on a second," Raiden interjected,

putting his hands up to keep Jack and Firestar from killing each other. "Why else would Jack come tell us about the attack? Would you have him drag her own of bed after she's had such a fright?"

Firestar's nostrils flared as he inhaled the scent of the room. "She wasn't too frightened to let this one here between her thighs."

"Not that it is any of your business," Jack calmly stated, crossing his arms over his chest. "But wasn't it you two who wanted us to get on with it in the first place?"

"But not while she was in danger." Firestar stepped toward Jack anger filling his face. "You could have been attacked with your pants down."

Jack snorted. "I do not know about you, but I can handle myself just fine with or without my pants."

Now the conversation was just getting ridiculous. Men would argue in circles about something they didn't even know about until someone came in to end it. It looked like it would have to be me.

"Guys," I said from the bathroom door. "I'm fine. Jack's fine. He didn't do anything I didn't want, so stop badgering him." I gestured at the ice dragon, who smirked. "Besides, isn't it more important to find out who tried to attack me?"

"Agreed," Jack nodded.

"I guess so." Raiden ran a hand through his hair with a sigh.

Firestar didn't say anything, his hard gaze staring at something off into the distance. The tight clenching of his jaw told me he wasn't happy with any of the events and maybe even mine and Jack's union. I hoped his anger was for the attack and not the latter, but who knew what was going on in that hot head of his.

"Not that I'm not enjoying the view," Raiden said, his eyes sliding up and down my form with an appreciative grin. "But I think you should put some clothes on before we are late."

Frowning at him as I approached, I asked, "Late for what?"

My nude form aside, I didn't like the way Raiden was looking at Jack and me. He was far too pleased with himself as if our actions had been all his doing. Or maybe he was just happy to see his family? Hard to tell with him, he'd laugh at his own fart.

"You guys finally did it," Raiden explained, grinning from ear to ear. "And you know what that means?" Raiden clapped Jack on the back and pointed toward the door. "To the training yard."

The training grounds at Raiden's home weren't very different from ours back home, except for one difference. All along the fence posts were large metal spikes. They looked dangerous and more likely to get someone killed than help with training.

"Raiden," I asked when we arrived next to the menacing points. "What's with the spikes? If you are just training, won't they raise the chances of injury?"

Raiden glanced at the metal spikes and shrugged. "I've never had any issue with them before, but they aren't just there for looks. We're lightning dragons, what's the point of having the powers if we can't practice using them?"

"So, they are used as conduits?" I asked, wanting to be away from them even more. Sharp points and a strong source of lightning, not a good mix. Sure, my power lay in the Earth and lightning wouldn't do much but give me a bad hair day. But still, better safe than sorry.

"Pretty much," Raiden answered but didn't elaborate as his brothers approached. "So, who wants a piece of me first?"

"Me," Raijin answered, pulling a long staff with a pointed end from the weapons rack. He swung it around with experienced ease before striking a pose.

I couldn't help but smile at how overdramatic the lightning dragons were. Really, it was a fight, not a beauty contest.

"Not so fast," Firestar interrupted before they could get into the ring. "The whole point of coming down here was to see what Jack had to offer, not to watch you peacocks dance around each other all day."

The lightning brothers glanced over at Jack with questioning eyes, but Raiden knew what Firestar meant. Sighing with regret, Raiden turned to Jack. "I guess I can warm up with you and then destroy my brothers."

Raijin scoffed as Fujin said, "Like hell, you will."

"I could mop the floor with you right now," Raiden claimed and brought forth his magic until his trident formed in his hands. His brothers' eyes widened, and a flash of fear crossed their faces before it was replaced with envy.

"Enough," Firestar snapped before the brothers could get into it again. "I will be fighting Jack. You can fight the loser, and then we can decide from there."

Not at all happy with the decision, Raiden

nodded tightly and moved to the side, dismissing his trident for the time being.

Jack, who hadn't said a word one way or the other, approached the training field with confidence. We didn't know what kind of powers he would receive from being with me or if he'd even get any at all, but if he was worried, he didn't look it. Jack removed his jacket and glanced around for somewhere to put it.

"Here," I offered, holding my hands out. Jack paused for a moment before handing it over with a soft smile. Those small curl of his lips were special and only reserved for me. I'd never get tired of seeing it.

With his jacket in my arms, I resisted the urge to bring it to my nose to inhale his scent. Though, I needn't have bothered. The smell of him wafted up to my nose. Just that was enough to cause my body to respond in kind. Even though I ached, I still wanted him inside me again, and the way he arched a brow at me told me he knew it.

Refusing to acknowledge the power he now had over my libido, I moved over to stand by Raiden, who had no problem throwing his arm over my shoulders and pulling me close. Not that it helped matters, but it kept me from feeling so out of control of my body. I hadn't even felt this way when Raiden and I had first had sex. Maybe size did matter.

Not bothered by my actions, Jack moved into position opposite of Firestar. The fire dragon pulled his magic into his hands forming his kusarigamas in his palms. The lightning brothers made appreciative sounds but didn't comment as we all waited to see what would happen next.

Jack's hands began to glow like they always did when he called on his powers, but they didn't form into a weapon like the others. Frowning, I glanced up at Raiden and whispered so his brothers couldn't hear us, "What do you think is wrong?"

"I don't know." He shrugged. "But mine didn't come out until mid-battle when those men were attacking you, and Firestar's came out while we were fighting over you. Maybe they need to start fighting for it to happen?"

"Maybe," I answered, but I wasn't so sure. We'd been lucky so far but what if this was when our luck had finally run out? What if I didn't have as much magic in me as everyone thought? Two power boosts might just be my limit.

"What are you waiting for?" Firestar shouted at

Jack, swinging his kusarigamas around in his hands. "Do it already!"

"Do you not think I am trying?" Jack countered with a frustrated growl. "Nothing is happening."

"Just start fighting," Raiden called out from the sidelines. "Maybe it needs to warm up first."

Jack and Firestar glanced to Raiden and then nodded in agreement. Then without warning, Firestar came at Jack. Snowflake covered wings sprouted from Jack's back as he jumped out of the way of Firestar's attack. Hovering in the air, he spun around and lashed out with his ice-covered fist.

Firestar blocked it with his kusarigama, making Jack pull back with a wince. Not waiting for Jack to attack again, Firestar sprouted his own wings. Made of pure fire, they glowed hot red and yellow as he took to the sky. I craned my neck to follow their movements and wished once more for my own set of wings.

"It's not working," Raiden said, pulling me from my envious thoughts. "Jack should have been able to create something by now."

Frowning at his assessment, I tried to remember how Raiden had gotten his new powers. Six fire dragons had ambushed our camp. Jack and Raiden had been too busy fighting multiple ones to help me when one of them attacked. He'd almost got me too if Raiden hadn't gotten there in time to save me.

"What did you think about before yours showed up?" I asked, glancing up at him.

Brow furrowed, Raiden's lips pressed together in thought. "I wasn't thinking of anything really, I just knew I wanted to save you."

"And what about Firestar?" I shot my eyes back up to the sky. "What happened right before his formed?"

"We were arguing," Raiden explained without hesitation. "I told him he wasn't worthy of you and that he'd only get you killed. Then he attacked me."

"So, the need to protect me is what caused your powers to come to life," I mused aloud, not really paying any mind to the brothers any longer. Even if they did figure out what we were talking about, Raiden had assured me they weren't a threat, but someone was. Someone had broken into my room with the intentions of hurting me. It gave me an idea.

Jack was losing badly. He was barely keeping up with Firestar's attacks. Even his shirt had started to smolder and burn from where he hadn't blocked well enough. But I hoped to change the tide with my next words.

"Jack," I shouted as he came close to our side of the ring. "You're never going to protect me the way you are now."

His pale eyes darted to where I stood briefly before turning back to barely block one of Firestar's kusarigamas. Aware that my words were working, I moved away from Raiden's grasp and toward the field. Wrapping my hands around the fence, I leaned in so my voice would be heard.

"What would have happened if they'd still been there? The men that ransacked my room?" I asked, making sure to make my voice sound fragile and worried. "Would you have been able to protect me? Or if there had been more than one? Do you think the way you are now would have been enough?"

Jack's eyes locked on me once more this time their color liquid steel. I'd touched a nerve. Good. Firestar glanced my way and then with a smirk realized what I was doing.

"You're weak," Firestar growled, lashing out with his fiery weapons. "Too weak to keep her safe, too weak to be in her bed, and far too weak to father her child." Each point was punctuated with another attack until all Jack could do was defend.

For a moment, I thought my idea had been stupid, that it wouldn't do any good and Jack would get the shit end of the stick. But then the temperature dropped, and my breath came out in puffs of white clouds. I felt Raiden move closer to me as the air thickened with magic.

"It's happening," Raiden murmured next to me. I nodded but didn't answer my attention solely on the fight before me.

Frost spread across Jack's form so that the next hit by Firestar smacked against solid ice. The kusarigamas bounced off him, and this time Firestar stopped to watch. Now that the ice was no longer defending him, it moved through him to settle in his hand. My eyes widened as a long thick handle formed in his hand, the end of it forming a large war hammer. His hand flexed around the handle and drew it up in front of him.

Made of pure ice, I could see straight through it as it glistened in the light. Snowflakes decorated the core of the hammer, reminding me of his gorgeous wings. I wondered if it was as heavy as it looked.

After a moment of reverence for his new weapon, Jack gestured at Firestar with a hand, taunting the fire dragon to come at him again. This time the battle was more even. Firestar had lighter weapons, so he should have been faster, but Jack swung the warhammer like it weighed nothing.

It took little to no time at all for Firestar to miss and get hit square in the chest by the hammer. The blow resounded across the training grounds as Firestar flew backward, smashing into the ground like a fiery comet. As Jack landed beside him, his hammer at the ready, Firestar waved a hand, conceding.

"Firestar never concedes," I gasped in awe of what I'd just seen. "He's too stubborn and prideful to give up unless he's in the ground."

"Looks like our boy has finally met his match," Raiden chuckled and practically bounced in place. I could feel the excitement roll off him in waves. He clearly couldn't wait to be in the ring and try Jack out for himself.

Jack approached us, his hammer swung over his shoulder and a bored expression on his face. "Who's next?"

"My turn," Raiden said with an overeager grin. He jumped into the training yard, and I prepared for what could be the biggest battle I'd ever witnessed. I just hoped there would be something left of them at the end.

12

At the end of the fight, slow clapping kept us from celebrating that they were even alive. Everyone turned to find the Lady of the East approaching with what I could only assume was her handmaiden.

"Mother," Raiden and his brothers said in unison, the fight no longer the priority. The sons scrambled over themselves to meet her before she reached the training yard.

"You've grown quite a lot during your time away," Lady Nariko stated, placing her hands on Raiden's face. "You might even be stronger than your brothers now."

Raiden smiled like a fool and rubbed the back of his head. "Well, I don't know about that, but I've had some time to train while they've bickered like children."

"Hey," Raijin shouted, coming up next to Raiden. "That's not fair. While we were keeping our lands safe, you've been plunging your sword into this one." He pointed at me and then quickly added, "No offense, my lady."

"None taken." I waved him off. I didn't care what they said as long as they didn't ask about the guys' powers. I wasn't sure what'd we do to explain how they got those. I had a sudden surge of regret for rushing to see Jack's powers. We were idiots to do it here where anyone could see. We should have waited until we were outside the city walls where no one would question us.

Lady Nariko simply smiled at her boys the way a mother did when she knew they were being silly. "You have all done well, and I am proud of you all. But, Raiden, my son, I have to wonder…" she trailed off as her gaze landed me "Where did you learn such abilities?"

"What do you mean?" Raiden asked, he took a step back from his mother, his eyes skittering across the ground. Well, we knew who wasn't a liar in our group. Raiden might as well have shouted it to the world that his powers were a secret for all his reaction did.

"I mean," his mother continued, moving her intense gaze back to her youngest son. "Those are not common abilities. In fact, there are few I've ever heard of being able to manifest their magic into solid objects and here we are with not one but three different dragons all wielding magnificent weapons of destruction. You can't fault me for wondering where such powers came from."

"While we were working to create an heir, we had not much else to do but train. Of course, grueling hours in the training yards would yield great results." Firestar tried to save us, but I could tell by Lady Nariko's expression that nothing he said would change her mind.

"I doubt it," was the only response Lady Nariko made. She moved past her son and stopped in front of me. Dark eyes locked on mine as her hand caught my chin within her grasp. Moving my face this way and that she seemed to be searching for an answer. One I knew I would not give her.

"Mother," Raiden stepped in, placing a hand on her shoulder. "Release Maya, this has nothing to do with her."

"Oh, I think it does," his mother purred but

released my face all the same. I refused to rub my chin where her pincer like nails had poked me. She seemed the kind to get off on other people's misery. She and my father would make quite the pair, should they ever meet.

"What are you talking about?" Fujin asked finally taking an interest in where the conversation was going. "How could a woman have anything to do with their powers? Only intense training and time on the battlefield could cause such a boost in power. Right?" Fujin glanced at his brother Raijin, who shrugged in answer.

"It's been said that a true mate can complete a dragon in ways that no one else could. A force to be reckoned with," Lady Nariko explained, her eyes scanning over the four of us. "That their love could grow into a monstrous amount of power, enough to conquer all of Waesigar, if they so wished."

Lady Nariko's explanation blew me away. The thought that we could become some unstoppable force didn't seem possible. I could hardly fight my own battles let alone take over the whole world.

"And you think Maya has done such a thing with them?" Fujin nodded to me, wonder and confusion on his face. "How can that be?"

Lady Nariko shrugged. "I've only ever heard of

it happening between two people. Those two halves completing a whole so to speak but to cause such a change in not one but three men? Now that is something else entirely." Her eyes lit with a fire that made me take a step back. It wasn't fear or anger I saw in there but want.

Lady Nariko didn't want me sexually, but she coveted my power, I could see it in her eyes. If not for herself than for her kingdom. It was Firestar's camp all over again, and the very thing I feared would happen. If she told anyone, then I would be even more of a target than I already was. I could already tell that wouldn't bother her. Even if her son loved me. She wanted power, and I had little doubt she would stop at anything to get it.

"Now," Lady Nariko sighed and fanned herself slightly. "All this excitement is a bit too much for an old lady like me. I think I'll go lie down."

"Of course," Raiden hurried to help his mother over to her handmaiden. Lady Nariko might be a lot of things, but she knew how to play her sons. The weak, fragile facade would only go so far with me. I'd only been playing the game for a short amount of time, and I could already find those who were playing it too. And the Lady of the East played it well.

"Don't forget," she added as she let her hand-maiden guide her toward the palace. "Your father wanted to meet with you later today. Don't keep him waiting."

"Yes, mother," the three lightning princes answered at once.

Their mother had her claws firmly in them, and I didn't know how I would get them out. My own mother was lovely if a bit of a pushover when it came to my father. Seeing what they had to deal with I was thankful for my own. I couldn't deal with two overbearing parents, even if one of them was a bit slyer about it.

"What are we going to do?" I hissed when we got back to Jack's room. My room was still being cleaned up the door still hadn't been replaced. I hadn't even had the chance to ask Raiden's family about the attack.

"About what?" Raiden asked as he flopped down in a chair by Jack's dresser.

I exchanged an exasperated look with Jack and Firestar, pleading for them to help me out before I crushed all of Raiden's hopes and dreams. I was not going to be the one who told him his mother was a power-hungry viper.

"Raiden," Jack started his voice in his usual

emotionless tone. "I believe Maya is worried your mother might let our little secret slip."

"She wouldn't do that," Raiden jumped up from his seat, shaking his head. "I told you before they could be trusted, and I meant it. She wouldn't do anything that would hurt me and hurting you would hurt me." Raiden grabbed my hands a self-assured look on his face.

I wanted to believe him but too many years with my father had taught me better. His mother couldn't be trusted. His brothers were too dumb to even think of trying to get powers from me and his father - well his father was married to Lady Nariko. There was no telling if he was aware of his wife's power-hungry tendencies or if she had hidden it from him.

"Still," I rubbed Raiden's arms trying to sound conversational and not at all accusing. "I would feel better if we didn't show any more of your powers while you were in the palace walls. All right?"

"Fine," Raiden sighed and then added, "But I'm not holding back when we go on the raid later today."

"Raid?" I raised a brow and glanced at Firestar and Jack for some answers. "What raid?"

This time Firestar answered, "We finally

convinced the brothers to agree to my plan. We are going to draw the raiders into one of the smaller villages and then take them by surprise. Then we will get to the bottom of who's been attacking the Eastern lands."

I chewed on my bottom lip not liking the thought of them putting themselves in danger. There had been raids all over the world, not just in the East but who was behind them was anyone's guess. The raiders didn't exactly wear anyone's colors or symbols. For all we knew, it could be unaligned dragons attacking the other regions just because they could.

"All right," I finally said, marching for the door. "The sooner we get this over with, the sooner we can find out who attacked me."

When I opened the door, and the guys didn't follow I stopped. Turning on my heel, I placed my hands on my hips and scowled. "What's the problem?"

"We don't think you should go," Raiden answered, a guilty frown on his lips. He rubbed the back of his head and kicked the ground with the toe of his boot. "It will be pretty dangerous, and it would be just us guys so—"

"So, I'd just be in the way is what you are

saying, isn't it?" I growled, crossing my arms over my chest.

"We aren't saying that at all," Jack tried to explain, but then Firestar interrupted.

"Speak for yourself," He grunted and when I turned my hurt eyes to him added, "We don't want you to get hurt, Maya. You're still rusty, and this is serious."

"And you don't think I can help?" I countered, my eyes brimming with tears. "What's the point of teaching me to fight better if I can't put it to use? Did you think before all this I just sat around at home while the others fought?"

"Of course not," Raiden said and tried to take me into his arms, but I shook him off.

Anger fueled me at their treatment. I might not be the strongest of them, but I still could fight. My magic vagina wasn't the only thing I was good for.

"Stop that right now," Jack demanded, pulling me from my thoughts. "We all care for you and wouldn't tell you to stay here if we didn't have a good reason. No one is saying you are worthless, but this is a sensitive mission."

"Exactly," Raiden agreed and then placed his hands on my shoulders rubbing in soothing circles. "You'll be safer here," Raiden reassured me, and I gave him an incredulous glare. "Well, safer than out there. I can have a guard posted at your door. Plus." He gestured at my stomach with a frown. "You're supposed to be pregnant. Can't have you gallivanting all over the region."

"He is right," Firestar said, nodding. "I don't like leaving you here alone. Especially after what happened last night, but we can't bring you with us, and we can't stay here. Our hands are tied."

I sighed and glanced at Jack, hoping he would have a better option. The ice dragon took my hand in his and caressed my face with the other one. "I am sorry, Maya, but it is for the best. Stay in your room or find Lady Nariko and stay by her side."

I snorted at that suggestion. I would be even less safe near that harpy. I kept my thoughts to myself, not wanting to hurt Raiden's feelings. One's parents could be a hard spot to poke at, and I didn't want to hurt our relationship. Raiden would have to learn on his own what kind of woman his mother truly was, and if the way she looked at me earlier was any indication, I had a feeling she would show her true face soon enough.

13

Pacing didn't make waiting any better. If anything, it made it worse. I'd already created a path in the rug from my pacing, and if it didn't find something soon to distract myself, I was going to go crazy.

But what to do? The guys had told me to stay in the room unless I sought out Raiden's mother. I rolled my eyes and stuck out my tongue in disgust. Like that would ever happen.

I might have to deal with her for Raiden's sake, but that didn't mean I was going to go out of my way to seek out that horrid woman. I had little doubt she was plotting how best to exploit my abilities or rather her son's abilities. I shook my head in shame.

I barely knew the woman and had no right to criticize her or her motives. Just because I was assuming didn't mean I was right. Though, if I wasn't right about Lady Nariko, I'd eat my left shoe.

Stopping mid-pace, I glanced around the room for something to distract me from thinking of that foul woman. My eyes settled on Jack's dresser, and a naughty part of me snickered. I strolled across the room and placed my hands on Jack's dresser. Pausing, I had a moment of guilt. I shouldn't look through his things, it wouldn't be right.

Then again, they had left me here with nothing to do while they go off saving the kingdom. Could the guys really fault me for getting bored? They were lucky I wasn't getting drunk and running around naked, which I had longed to do since I arrived home and could actually get drunk. Sadly, my lie had made that impossible.

Pulling the top drawer open, my heart beat rapidly in my chest. I felt like a child getting presents for the first time. Except when I dug into the draw, I felt like the child who only got socks when they really wanted the hottest toy of Christmas season.

I should have known better than to expect

anything naughty in my ice dragon's drawers. He was far too sophisticated for that. However, my eyes darted to the nightstand. Perhaps he wasn't completely a stick in the mud.

Ripping the drawer open, I pulled a bit too hard, making the contents fall all over the ground. My eyes shot to the bedroom door, expecting Jack or the guys to come bursting through at any moment.

When no one did, I knelt on the ground beside the bed searching my treasures. I picked up a dark-colored book and glanced at the spine. My brows rose in surprise when I realized it was a romance novel. A red bookmark stuck out of the side and when I opened it my brows shot even higher.

My eyes skimmed the words on the page, my skin getting heated at the steamy scene on the pages. A deep ache developed between my thighs and I hurried to close the book before I got too excited. Who knew when the guys would be back to help me itch my scratch?

Putting the book aside, I picked up the rest of the things that had fallen. A hairbrush, a pale blue ribbon that I could just imagine in Jack's hair. When I finished picking up everything and putting it back in its place, I moved to stand up, but a glinting under the bed stopped me.

Kneeling back down, I reached under the bed. My fingers wrapped around cool metal and I withdrew it with interest. A dagger with an ornate silver handle. A bright blue sapphire was fitted into the pommel, and without even touching the short blade, I knew it was razor sharp.

Fingering the dagger, I stood. I wondered where he had gotten it. Maybe a family member? Or a lover? Jealousy flared up at the thought. It was silly to worry about past lovers when Jack was here with me now, but the blade was obviously meant for a woman. Chewing my cheek, I flipped the blade over in my hand as I contemplated the possibilities that Jack might have a lover back home.

My heart ached at the thought and my eyes pricked with emotion. Thankfully, before I could go down the spiraling slop of misery, there was a knock at the door.

I stuck the dagger in my boot, careful of the tip and then marched over to the door. Behind it stood a nervous young man. He couldn't have been older than sixteen. His eyes met mine briefly, and his ears and face turned redder than Firestar's hair.

"M-my lady," he stuttered and half-bowed. "Lady Nariko has requested you have tea with her."

Forcing back the immediate rejection on the tip of my tongue, I sighed. I had wanted something to do, and while I hadn't sought Lady Nariko out, it couldn't hurt to see what Lady of the East wanted, maybe I'd been wrong about her? One could only hope. Before I could decide one way or the other, my stomach decided to growl its vote.

The teen before me blushed even harder, eyes flicking to my stomach. I laughed and put him out of his misery. "Very well, lead the way."

By the time we arrived at the Lady of the East's rooms, I was questioning my sanity. Had I really agreed to have tea with the woman who hated me? Sure, her sons were wonderful, her youngest in particular, but how those three came from such a horrible woman mystified me.

Before I could back out, my blushing guide had taken off, leaving me at the open door he had already knocked on. A voice from inside beckoned me in, and I took a deep breath before letting it out. Be nice. For Raiden's sake.

"Maya," Lady Nariko cooed as I came through the doors. Her room was set up more like my parents with a small sitting room for guests in front of a door that led to the bedroom. A cute table and chairs were set next to balcony doors which were thrown open to bring in the air. If my nose could be trusted, we were going to have rain soon. Not that it meant much since it seemed to always be raining here.

"Lady Nariko," I greeted, taking the seat, she gestured to. I felt underdressed sitting across from her in my jeans and t-shirt. Lady Nariko, on the other hand, looked every bit the ruler she was in her long green skirt and high-necked blouse. Even her dark hair had been twisted into a delicate up-do that could have been a crown in its own right.

Forcing a smile onto my face, I picked up my already steaming teacup. "Thank you for inviting me. I was simply going mad in my room."

Lady Nariko chuckled and sipped from her own cup. "I can imagine. We women have to keep busy when we're left behind."

I tried not roll my eyes. "Sadly, I'm not used to being left behind. I'd rather be in the middle of the fight than sitting on the sidelines. Even worse sitting at home and not even getting to see what is going on."

"Yes, well," Lady Nariko started a sly smile covering her lips. "When we carry precious cargo, we must make sacrifices. You are pregnant, aren't you?" A delicate brow rose, but I had a feeling she already knew the answer.

"Yes, of course," I murmured into my cup, not meeting her scrutinizing gaze. After a moment, I cleared my throat and opened my mouth to change the subject. Before I could, Lady Nariko sat her cup down with a loud thwack.

"Let's stop pretending here," she quipped and laced her fingers in front of her. Her dark eyes on me had a sharp edge to it. "I know you aren't pregnant, and I also know that until recently, you hadn't mated with all the men in your entourage."

Mouth agape, it took me a second to find my words before they tumbled out, "I'm sorry, I don't know what you are talking about."

"Oh, please stop it." Lady Nariko waved me off and shifted in her seat. "We are both grown women here." She leaned forward with a conspiratorial gleam in her eyes. "Let's be honest, you aren't very good at lying."

Instead of answering, I chugged my tea even though it burned my tongue. Taking a deep breath, I settled into my seat and met Lady Nariko with a stern look of my own. "What do you want?"

"See." Lady Nariko pointed at me with one

finger as she picked her cup back up with the other hand. "That wasn't so hard, was it? Now, let's get down to business."

I didn't like the sound of that. Lady Nariko held all the cards, and I wished I knew what she planned to do with them. I reminded myself it couldn't be any worse than what my own father had done to me. I hoped.

"You must have some reason for pretending to be pregnant."

"I—" I tried to interrupt and explain, but she waved me off.

"Honestly, I don't care about your reasons. All I care about is what you have going on down there in those ridiculous pants." Her eyes shifted to my lap underneath the glass table. I shifted in my seat and crossed my legs over one another.

"Excuse me?"

"Please don't play coy," Lady Nariko sniffed. "We both know that your men didn't just come into their new abilities because of intense training or whatever other nonsense you four are spouting. I've read the histories enough to know what you have is rare."

"True love is always hard to find," I interrupted, trying to remind her of the reasoning she and her sons had talked about before. If she believed it was only because we cared about each other so much, then she wouldn't be able to use me. Which hopefully would spread around to the rest of the kingdom, and I would have one less target on my back.

"So, you love my son?" She raised a mocking brow at me as she poured me another glass of tea. I opened my mouth to answer, but she cut me off once more. "Of course, you do. Why wouldn't you? My son is a remarkable man, and he makes you laugh. But did you love him before you two fucked?"

I choked on my second cup of tea, not expecting this perfectly put together lady to curse so freely. "I don't really think that's any of your business."

"Oh, pish posh." If she waved me off one more time, I swore I was going to cut her hand off with the blade still in my boot. "Do you think you are the first dragoness to mess around with men they didn't care for?" Lady Nariko snorted and rolled her eyes. "There'd never be any children running around if we waited for true love."

Getting irritated at the direction of the conversation, in the whole thing really, I barely held back the bite in my voice. "I hope you have a point to this in there somewhere?"

"Good," Lady Nariko patted on the table. "You are finally getting serious."

This time I kept my mouth shut and just waited for her to tell me what the hell she wanted.

"Seeing as we already established that true love didn't create those astounding new powers your men have, I don't see why you couldn't give them to my other two sons." A nasty sort of laughter covered her face making her eyes crinkle at the sides.

"Excuse me?" I didn't know why I asked. I knew what she meant, who she meant, but I needed to hear it from her lips. To solidify the kind of woman I thought her to be.

"Dreq and Aido, of course." She rolled her eyes. "Those are their real names, if you didn't know."

"I did, but I still don't know what you mean," I replied, looking down at my cup.

"What I mean is this. You already gave those powers to Raiden," she explained like I was an idiot. "You can do the same for my other two boys. They will take some convincing, but you are a lovely woman, and I'm sure they will come around once they find out the benefits." She gestured up and down my person as if having sex with me would be a job they would have to grin and bear to get the big payout.

"No," I clipped with a shake of my head. "Absolutely not."

A flash of irritation filled Lady Nariko's eyes before it was gone. Sighing, she stood from her seat and reached over the table to take my hands.

"I understand. You are worried about what your men will think. But the way I see it, if they were willing to share you with two other men, they should be willing to do this. Of course." She let me go and sat back down. "I will provide ample compensation. I hear your Firestar is quite in need of the money." An evil glint twinkled in her eyes as a smug grin covered her lips. "I have lots of money at my disposal."

How did she know all this? Did she have spies all over Waesigar? She even knew what was going on in my own bedroom. I was half-tempted to make sure there wasn't a bug in my pants.

"Listen," she sighed after I didn't immediately jump on her offer. "Take a few days to think about it. It's a big decision. I understand. Nevertheless, don't take too long deciding or a letter disclosing all your secrets might just find its way to every Lord in Waesigar, including your father."

Hot fury filled me at her threat. If she thought I would just lay back and spread my legs because she said so, she had another thing coming. I didn't care if she told my father about my lies. I'd tell him my damned self before I'd ever consider doing her other two sons.

Hands balled into fists, I prepared myself to tell her exactly that, but then a dragon messenger came shooting through the balcony doors. Out of breath and covered in dirt, the messenger turned to Lady Nariko. "The attack."

"What of it?" Lady Nariko asked, impatient to send him away.

"There were more raiders than they anticipated and..."

"You are saying they are outnumbered?" I finished for him, my heart pounding in my chest. The messenger nodded quickly. The world spun around me as I tried to comprehend what the dragon before me had said. All three of my men were out there right now fighting for this horrid woman's kingdom, and here she was demanding I screw her sons.

All my rage funneled through my body and my

magic built with it. I knew if I didn't let it out, it would end up hurting me or someone else. I knew one person I'd love to use it on, but I also knew if Raiden survived that he would never forgive me.

So, with nowhere else to go, the power built in my chest until it found an outlet. Through my back.

14

Wings, I had wings. They spread out of my back and lifted me slightly into the air.

I angled my head to see over my shoulder but could barely take in the pale green of my newfound wings. Excitement replaced my anger, and I searched the room for a mirror. When my eyes landed on a long mirror decorating the wall, I rushed over to it before I could stop myself. Or rather flew.

Without me thinking about it, my wings had moved on their own, flapping up and down and blowing my hair slightly as I moved. When I stopped in front of the mirror, I got an eyeful of them. Green as the bushes in my favorite garden back home, the veins of them looked like the vines I used to train with. Between each vein lay a spiral that could have been a flower blooming. They were remarkable, and I couldn't have asked for better.

Instantly, I wished for a full-length mirror, but knew I wouldn't be able to get to one until I got back to my room. Spinning around, I turned back to the other two people in the room. My face fell when I remembered why I had finally gotten my wings.

So, astounded by my new wings I didn't even notice Lady Nariko or the messenger staring at me like I'd lost my mind. My lighter than air feeling sunk, and so did my body. My feet hit the floor as I made my way back to the tea table.

"I have to go," I said, bypassing them and going to the balcony.

Lady Nariko and the messenger followed after me as I exited the palace and walked into the light sprinkle of rain.

"What are you doing?" Lady Nariko asked absolute horror on her face. "You can't mean to go after them?"

"I do," I said without apology. "I can't stand by while they fight. They could be dying right now or worse."

"But what will people say?" she argued, grabbing my arm her nails digging into my arm. "You're pregnant, you can't be seen going out there. People will talk."

"They'll say I care about the fathers of my child." I jerked my arm out of her grasp and took to the sky, leaving a screeching Lady of the East behind me.

Moving through the sky, the rain sprinkling down on me, it seemed like a dream. Of course, I'd hoped I'd be in the training yard or even better among my suitors when I finally got my wings. Sprouting them because of my worry for their safety seemed a tad bit too selfless for me. Finally getting them to spite my father? Sure. Even getting them to save me from a sudden fall off a cliff sounded more plausible.

Apparently, my dragoness decided I wasn't worthy of them until someone I loved really needed me. Too bad those someones were miles away, and I had no idea where I was going.

Just outside the city gates, I tried to pause in mid-air to figure out where I was going, but instead of pausing, my wings quit flapping altogether. Plunging out of the air, a scream ripped from my throat as the ground came closer and closer to my view.

"Up, up!" I commanded my wings. When they didn't so much as flutter, I covered my face with my arms and called on my magic seeking something out of the earth to make a cushion for my fall. The ground billowed up into a mound of thick grass, but before I could land on it, my wings suddenly came back to life, jerking me back up into the air.

Grumbling about stupid wings, I almost fell again before I cried out, "I'm sorry all right. Stop."

My wings were a sensitive bunch, much like my inner dragoness. She never let me do anything I wanted without my rolling over and begging. Even when we were in extreme danger. Just another pain in the butt to add to my long list of people to please other than myself.

Now that my wings were listening to me, I searched around the perimeter, looking for some sign of where the guys had gone off to. I remembered Firestar pointing at the large replica of the area. There had been a village not too far from the castle, small and near a small river.

I spun in a circle lifting myself higher and higher until I could see the barest glimpse of water. I followed the line of the river until it hit a bundle of trees. If I squinted my eyes, I could make out the tops of a few houses and what's more smoke.

There. That had to be it.

My pulse sped up as I focused on flying in that direction. My still new wings ached from overuse. My breathing came in hard pants, and I gritted my teeth, determined to make it there in time. I wouldn't lose them like this. I couldn't.

As if knowing my plight, the sky opened, and a downpour of rain hit me. Not prepared for the weather's onslaught, I lost my momentum as the water hit my fresh baby wings. The ground came closer to me as I lost altitude. If I landed, I wasn't sure I'd make it back up again.

Pushing forward, I barely hovered above the ground as I shoved through the trees surrounding the village. Clashing of swords and the prickle of magic hit me minutes before I cleared the tree line. My feet hit the ground as my wings gave out on me, followed by my heart.

The sight before me had my blood running cold. Bodies littered the ground, lightning dragons and ones I didn't recognize. Blood became streams as the rain mixed with it as it flowed downhill toward the river. The only positive side was none of the bodies I could see were familiar to me.

"Jack! He's getting away." My head whipped toward the voice. Firestar. And Jack if his words had anything to say about it. But what about Raiden?

My feet began to move on their own, the need to know they were okay overwhelming any survival instinct I might have had. Rounding a burning house, I found myself in the thick of battle. Magic and steel flew through the air, and I almost ended up with my head chopped off for my negligence.

Grabbing the dagger I'd taken from Jack's things, I dodged an attack and slashed out, catching the raider who had attacked me in the stomach. He fell to the ground clutching his wound, but I didn't stay to see if he died. My focus was entirely on finding my men.

A fireball shot out, and I rolled sideways away from it. I searched for the thrower, but Firestar was nowhere in sight. Fire dragons? That didn't make sense. Why were they all the way over here?

Before I could contemplate where to go next, the ground shifted beneath me. I braced myself and tried to counter the magic with my own but wasn't fast enough. Thrown off my feet, the ground rolled until it shoved me against an abandoned home. Breath knocked out of me but free of the ground's attack, I placed my hand on the wall as I tried to regain control of my lungs.

Not just fire dragons. Earth dragons. Immediately my father came to mind. My mother and sister had said something about making it so there were no more raids. Had this been what they were talking about? But that didn't explain why there were fire dragons here.

While I was lost in thought, I didn't sense the newcomer until the hand was on my shoulder. My hand instantly grabbed hold of it as I swung my leg out to hit whomever my attacker was.

"Stop," Raiden said, stepping back and avoiding my attack.

"Raiden!" I practically cried and relaxed my stance. Mud and blood covered, I'd never been happier to see the lightning dragon. Raiden's expression though didn't say the same.

"Maya, what are you doing here?" he growled, pulling me close to him as a flying bolt of lightning charred the ground beside us. "You were supposed to wait at home."

"I know, I know." I shook my head, my hands clutching his dirty shirt. "But a messenger came saying you guys were losing, and I couldn't stay behind. I just had to come to help."

"Well, we're pretty fucked. The earth dragons are canceling out most of our lightning powers. If it hadn't been for Jack and Firestar, we'd all be dead." His eyes went to the fighting men who were throwing bolts of lightning that dissipated harmlessly against the earth.

Scanning the area, I searched for the earth dragons. I might not be able to do much, but I could stop them. Then Raiden and his brothers could take the rest of them out. My magic sought out like magic. In an instant, my magic zeroed in on three men standing off to the side.

"There!" I pointed a finger at them, drawing Raiden's attention. "We have to take out those three. They're the earth dragons hindering your powers."

Raiden's trident flickered as he swung it through the air. Then he spat in anger. "I can't do it. Hell, I can't even get close to them. Their magic is pushing me back. You'll have to do it, Maya." He gave me a meaningful look, and I shook my head. "I know you can do it."

"I can't take on all three of those guys at once, they'll demolish me!"

Hands on my shoulders, Raiden hushed me. "You don't have to. Just take them out one at a time, but you'll have to be quick about it before the others notice. I'll provide backup so you can get to them without worry."

Taking a deep breath, I held the dagger tight in my hand and followed after Raiden. He led me around a house, until we were behind the earth dragons, bypassing the thickest part of the fighting. When we were only a few feet from the first one, Raiden motioned me to stop.

"All right, love." He waved me forward. "It's all you."

Dagger at the ready, I crept along the wall of the house until I came to the edge. The fighting wasn't as thick here so it would be hard for my movements to go unnoticed. I needed some kind of distraction.

"Raiden," I hissed, getting the lightning dragons attention. "See those two fighting over there? Right in front of my first guy?"

Raiden followed my gaze and nodded. "Say no more."

Shooting out from behind the house, he darted into the fray. The earth dragon near me saw Raiden as he thrust his trident into a raider. He focused his attention on him, giving me the chance to run out. Dagger poised, I reached into the earth. Pulling the roots up, I directed them to wrap about the earth dragon like a boa constrictor with its prey. The roots squeezed the man until his eyeballs bulged in his head. Before he could use his own powers to release himself, I shoved my dagger through his back and into his heart.

Jerking it free in a spray of blood, I watched his corpse collapse to the ground. Part of me was sickened by what I'd done, but most of me was satisfied.

One down, two to go.

Sprinting across the battlefield, I leapt through the air, calling upon my legs to give me a little bounce in my step. They burst from my back, flapping once, twice, three times, and giving me enough lift to carry me above the closest earth dragon as he turned toward where I'd been.

His eyes settled on his fallen friend, and as his face hardened, I slammed into him, smashing my knees into his collarbones. The bones snapped as he crashed to the ground beneath my weight, and as his head smacked against the earth with a wet smack, I drove the dagger into his eye, killing him.

I rose as his body twitched and spasmed, fastening my eyes on the last of the earth dragons. Only, as I saw him, my confidence fell away. The guy was looking right at me. Worse, Raiden was way too busy fighting off a horde of raiders to help.

The ground pulled out from beneath me, and I landed flat on my back. As I hurried to get back to my feet, the man charged at me. Shoving my powers into a nearby tree, I tried to get it to swing a limb out and knock him over. I must have overdone it though because the whole tree ripped from the earth, slamming into the earth dragon just as he reached me. The sound of snapping bone and breaking branches filled my ears as the weight of the huge tree turned him into a pancake.

Leaping to my feet, I called upon my powers to ensure the guy was dead.

"Raiden!" I shouted when I was sure the guy was dead. "You can use your powers now."

At the sound of my words, the air thickened and a huge bolt of lightning shot down from the sky, slamming into the men attacking Raiden. The men shuddered and screamed as they were fried from the inside out. Then one by one they fell to the ground as charred, smoking husks.

"You got them," I cried, running to his side.

Raiden pulled me into his arms, his mouth covering mine in a hard kiss before he leaned back and smiled. "No, you did it."

My own lips spreading out into a goofy grin, I couldn't help but feel a sense of pride. I had done it. Despite my doubts, I'd helped them!

The battle ended pretty quickly after that since the earth dragons were no longer dampening the majority of our fighters' magic. As we moved through the village, breaking up pockets of resistance, and helping our allies, I scanned the horizon for Firestar and Jack, but unfortunately, I didn't see them anywhere.

"What now? Should we look for the others?" I asked, searching around for a white or red head of hair.

Raiden's head shook from side to side, making his wet hair plastered to his face. Kissing my forehead, he smiled. "Well, nothing to be done now. Jack and Firestar had a bunch of them cornered over by the bridge, but these aren't the normal kind of raiders."

"I noticed," I admitted. "But I don't understand why they would come together to attack your people."

Raiden swung his trident and shoved it through an attacker behind me even before I knew he was there. "Unaligned is all we can figure, but we'll assess it more thoroughly after they're all dead."

Ducking and dodging attacks left and right we fought our way through the dwindling group of raiders. The few dozen Raiden's brothers had talked about were not even close to how many littered the village ground. There had to be fifty or more raiders, not counting those the lightning brothers had brought with them.

Worse, I knew they'd have been slaughtered by my men's new powers had they not been on the brothers' side.

"Firestar! Jack!" Raiden called out when we finally got out of the middle of the fray and to the bridge. The two dragons glanced away from their prisoners to Raiden. When their gazes landed on me, my blood froze. They were even less happy to see me than Raiden had been. I expected a lecture coming later, but now they were too busy with staying alive.

"What's she doing here?" Firestar snarled as he shoved his kusarigamas through one of the attackers. Blood splattered over him, and the others fell back. Raiden's brothers sat on the other side of the bridge keeping the others from getting away.

"I wanted to help," I answered for Raiden, returning Firestar's glare with one of my own. "I couldn't stand by and let you die."

"Do we look dead to you?" Firestar shouted in return, his anger obviously getting the best of him amongst the blood and chaos. "We can't take care of you right now."

"Hey, go easy on her," Raiden argued, patting me on the shoulder. "If it hadn't been for our girl, we wouldn't have won this one."

"Really?" Firestar asked not completely won over.

A man came up behind Firestar and Raiden cried out to warn him, but my borrowed dagger flew through the air and found its home in the man's face before Firestar could react. Eyes wide and mouth ajar, my three men stared at me like I'd done something unheard of. With a twist of my finger, the dagger jerked free of the man's face and returned to my hand.

"You were saying." I retorted, twirling the dagger in my hand.

Brow furrowed, Firestar turned his back on me and signaled to the lightning brothers. Raijin and Fujin had rounded up the last of the raiders and moved to capture the bridge.

The rain had slowed during the battle to barely a sprinkle, but it didn't help my hair plastered to my face and neck. I picked at it, trying to form it into some semblance of order, while blatantly ignoring Firestar. His eyes bore holes into my back, and then I realized no one had asked about my wings.

Reaching up, I grasped at my back only to touch air. Frowning, I wondered when they had disappeared. It must have been before Raiden found me because he hadn't said anything about them either. Too bad. It'd been nice to show them off. I wasn't sure if or when I'd be able to call them out again.

"You could have been killed," Firestar finally broke the silence, the anger barely contained in his voice.

"I wasn't," I countered.

"But you could have been." He pointed a kusarigama at me, the end of it sharp and gleaming. To an enemy, it would have made me think twice about talking back to him, but since I knew he wouldn't use it on me, it only made me roll my eyes.

"Regardless of popular belief, I was one of my father's best fighters." Though, no one would be able to tell now. Five years in banishment had done its job on my fighting skills. Being back in Waesigar hadn't helped that nor had my three overprotective suitors.

"I don't doubt that. I saw you fight before we

were separated, remember?" Firestar leaned against the edge of the bridge, crossing one ankle over the other. I raised a brow at his relaxed position when there were very dangerous men only feet behind him.

"I remember," I said, turning my attention back to him though danger still pricked at my senses. "You were mostly done fighting anyway, I don't know what the big deal is." I crossed my arms over my chest and shrugged.

"The big deal," Firestar repeated before leaning toward me so that we were inches apart. "The big deal is that not only did you put yourself and your men in danger, but you put our unborn child in danger."

I bent at the waist until my nose brushed his and murmured, "Our pretend unborn child you mean."

"Doesn't matter." Firestar shook his head, and his arm lashed out behind him, smacking a man who had gotten too close in the stomach. "They think you are, so if you want to keep up this ruse, then you have to act like it."

"I know," I grumbled, my lip poking out in a pout. Lady Nariko had said the same thing, and even though Firestar had repeated it, I knew she was right. Thinking of the Lady of the East made me remember what we had discussed just before I left.

"What is it?" Firestar asked, too observant for his own good.

I wanted to tell him, but one glance around us and I knew I couldn't, not here. There were too many ears and not enough allies. Giving Firestar a meaningful look, I said, "I'll tell you later."

Jack and Raiden came toward us keeping Firestar from questioning me further.

"Everything is taken care of," Raiden explained, gesturing back to the main part of the village. "Those who didn't die have been bound and are ready for transport back to the palace. Fujin! Raijin! Are you ready to go?"

His brothers called back their consent, and then the three dragons looked to me. "One of us will have to carry her, or it will take forever to get home. How did you get here in the first place?" Raiden asked, cocking his head to the side, so his bangs fell into his eyes.

I bounced on my heels and a goofy grin plastered across my lips. Finally, I got to tell them, and hopefully, if my wings cooperated, I could show them.

"I'm not sure I like that look on your face," Firestar grunted as I focused on my need to fly.

I watched their faces as my feet floated off the ground and their eyes widened. Doing a little spin mid-air which ended up being less of a twirl and more of a tumble before grabbing hold of Jack to keep my balance as I giggled. "I flew."

15

"How did this happen?" Jack asked, tracing along the edges of my wings and making a tingle run through me.

Shrugging my shoulders, I stared down at the ground as I recalled what happened. "When I found out you were outnumbered, I just knew I had to come help, but the only way I was going to get here in time was if I flew. So..." I waved a hand back at my wings as if they explained it all.

"So..." Raiden smirked and saddled up to me, his own wings sprouting up to let him hover beside me. "You finally got your wings because you were worried about us?"

Shoving a hand at him, I rolled my eyes and

giggled. "Don't get full of yourselves now. I just didn't think you could handle it on your own."

Firestar glanced around the scene and raised a brow. "I think we did all right."

"Only because I took a few out for you or you'd have gotten stabbed in the back," I pointed with the silver dagger. Jack's eyes locked on the blade and flushed. My first instinct had me putting it behind my back, but then I slowly withdrew it wiping the blood off before handing it to him hilt first.

"Where did you get this?" Jack asked, taking the dagger for me. He didn't seem mad, just confused.

I rubbed the back of my head as my feet touched the ground. "I found it."

"You found it?" Jack raised a perfectly arched brow his tone of voice telling me he didn't believe me.

"Okay." I sighed and threw my hands up in the air. "I snooped. I was going crazy waiting in your room, and I just couldn't take it anymore. If you really think about it, it's your fault for leaving me behind."

Hands on my hips, my lips puckered in a pout, I dared Jack to lecture me, but the ice dragon simply looked amused. It should have made me happy, but it only irritated me to no end. He thought I was funny? I'd show him funny.

"You know, if you're with me, then you need to be with me and not harbor a past lover's things." I pointed an accusatory finger at the dagger.

"Why would you think that?" Jack's face sobered and confusion took its place.

"Don't try to act innocent, buddy. That's a female dagger, don't try to deny it." I shoved a finger into his chest, getting worked up despite myself.

Firestar and Raiden shot looks at Jack as if they too were waiting for him to explain himself. His having a lover he hadn't been able to forget about would explain why he had been so reluctant to have sex with me right away like the others. But it didn't explain why he did now but still had the dagger.

"I won't deny it." Jack's hair swished around him as he shook his head. "It is a female's dagger, but it wasn't from a past lover."

"Then why do you have it?" Raiden asked this time, irritation in his own voice. It seemed my other suitors didn't care for cheating any more than I did. If he were going to be in this foursome, it would only be right for him to be in it wholeheartedly.

Jack sighed and rubbed his forehead as if he

were dealing with rowdy children. "The dagger is for you, Maya."

"For me?" my voice raised in pitch surprise filling it.

"Yes, for you." Jack nodded and handed the dagger back to me. "It was my mother's. I planned on giving it to you once we had consummated our relationship. But there never was a right time since then, so…"

"Oh." The one word was all I could say. I felt so embarrassed jumping to conclusions without letting him explain to me first. If I hadn't had snooped, then I wouldn't have found it leading to my embarrassing assumption.

Firestar cleared his throat saving me from having to say anything further. "Well, if we are done making asses of ourselves, I think we should get these prisoners back, so we can figure out who is behind their attacks."

Nodding in agreement, we took flight while the soldiers and the older brothers took care of getting the prisoners back. Since the rain had stopped, it was easier to get home than it had been on the way there. Also, I wasn't in such a hurry to get home which my wings thanked me for. While I loved being able to fly, I clearly needed more practice, so I wouldn't tire so easily.

Grateful to finally be back, I couldn't even argue when Firestar insisted I go rest while they dealt with the prisoners. I let myself be ushered back to our rooms, my eyes barely staying open from all the excitement.

"Are you going to be all right?" Raiden asked his hand on my elbow keeping me from going into the room. "I could stay with you if you need me. I'm sure the others can interrogate the raiders without me."

I placed my hand on Raiden's chest and leaned against his warm form. I wanted to tell him to stay just so I could curl up next to him while I napped, but I knew he really wanted to be there with the others. Pressing my lips to his in a chaste kiss, I gave him a small shove.

"Stop babying me. I can pass out all on my own thank you very much."

Raiden gave me a lopsided smile but then tucked my hair behind my ear, his fingers trailing along my face as they fell. I watched him walk away, my eyes lingering on his lower half longer than they should have.

Turning back to Jack's room, hand on the door

handle, I paused when I noticed something. Spinning back around, I stared at my room in shock. My door had been replaced. Could that mean they fixed my room?

Not that I didn't like sharing a room with Jack but having my own space was needed in a relationship as ours. Too many emotions with nowhere to go was hazardous to our health. It was a miracle none of us have beat the crap out of the other by now. We were bound for some kind of drama to occur soon. I just hoped it would wait until after I showered and took a nap.

The dagger Jack had given me in my hand, I slowly opened my door. Swinging it open, I half jumped into the room, prepared to attack first only to see my fully repaired bedroom. Letting out the breath I was holding, I made my way to the bathroom, my dagger still in my hand. When the coast was clear there, I pulled off my clothes which had become a second skin even after the rain had stopped, and stepped into the hot shower.

I didn't dally there this time. No matter how soothing the water may have been. My body ached, and my eyes were heavy. Washing my hair and body as quickly as I could, I jumped out of the shower only to find myself standing there like a dumbass. I didn't have any other clothing clean. The attacker had destroyed most of my room, and the clothes I had brought with me hadn't been replaced yet. We hadn't had time, and I didn't trust Raiden's mother to pick some for me.

Shrugging a shoulder, I was too tired to care about going to bed nude. Besides, only the guys would dare come in here will I slept. Dried off and ready for bed, I dropped the towel and slid under the covers. Burying myself deep into the pile of pillows, I was out before my eyes lids even fully closed.

Dreaming had never been something I did. When I did dream, I rarely remembered what I dreamt about. This time though, I jerked awake, my heart pounding and pulse racing as images of blood and fire filled the forefront of my mind. When I finally cleared my head and sat up, I realized I wasn't alone.

My eyes slowly raised from the bed to lock onto an unknown man. His clothes weren't of any alliance. He had dark hair and bright yellow eyes. The only interesting thing about him was the dagger in his hand. It was mine. I'd left it in the bathroom when I'd taken a shower.

"Do you mean to kill me with my own

weapon?" I asked, raising a brow and trying not to be bothered I sat naked in bed with a stranger staring down at me.

His eyes roamed over my figure clearly noticing my state of undress before he smirked. "Makes for easy cleanup. No witnesses and nothing left behind."

I forced myself to smile at him though I just wanted to scream my head off for help. "Understandable. So, before you kill me, who do I owe my death to?"

The man threw his head back and laughed. "I wouldn't be a very good assassin if I told you who my employer was."

"But I'll be dead anyway, who would I tell?" I shrugged a shoulder, letting the sheet fall slightly so that one of my breasts showed. The move had the desired effect, his eyes dipped down, locking on my exposed nipple. He licked his lips, and I could smell the scent of his arousal in the air, making my stomach roll. I shoved the feeling away.

He wanted me. Good. If I could keep him talking maybe, I'd have a chance to of killing him before he killed me.

Stroking his chin, he seemed to think about my offer. After a moment, he came to a decision and lowered the dagger. "Very well, I don't see the harm. Your cousin, Ned hired me to get rid of the competition. Families can be such a pain, can't they?"

I wished I could say I was surprised but after his attack in the gardens, it only made sense he'd try again. But I hadn't expected it so soon or through a third party. This guy didn't even look like one of ours.

If he had been hired by my cousin, then he wouldn't be easily paid off. Lucky for me I had more to bargain with than just gold. Crawling out from under the covers, I prowled toward the middle of the bed. The assassin's gaze followed me his lust almost choking my senses. I stopped when I had made it to the center and spread my legs so he could see all of me.

"My dear cousin didn't tell you why he wanted me dead, did he?" I asked, flipping my hair over my shoulder before trailing my fingers down my face and across my collarbone to cup my left breast.

The assassin licked his lips, his eyes firmly on my form. "Insurance. In case your father decided he still wanted you as his heir after Ned told him your little secret."

Ned had threatened to kill me if his original

plan didn't go the way he wanted. It seemed he'd gotten impatient to wait for me to return.

Anger at my cousin filled me as I wrapped my fingers around my nipple, I tugged on it for good measure before sighing. "It's too bad because I have something worth more than a crown."

"Oh yeah?" he cocked a brow and adjusted himself, his eyes following my hand as it dipped between my thighs. "I can see that."

With my fingers stroking, my eyes locked with his, a smug satisfaction filling me when I realized that I had him caught in my trap. "You must have heard the rumors about what I can give you?"

He shook his head and gave me a lopsided grin. "I don't believe in such fantasies or listen to common drivel."

"But it's true," I insisted with a breathy moan. "All those who lay with me end up with more power than they know what to do with, and you could have it. You could have it all." I spread my legs a bit wider on the last bit making sure he was good and focused on me before sliding from the bed.

Not bothering with the covers, I let my fingers trail the bed completely comfortable in my own skin. The assassin's eyes followed me, his gaze ravishing my skin with his lascivious thoughts. I placed my hand on the banister pole just a few feet away from him.

"What's to keep me from killing you right after I get these acclaimed powers?" The assassin fiddled with the dagger no longer holding onto it as well as he should have.

Shrugging one shoulder, I purred, "Nothing, but we can decide that afterward."

My mystery man chuckled and unbuckled his pants with one hand as he came toward me. So eager to take me he didn't even notice when I twitched my finger, pulling the blade from his hand and into my grasp. When he placed his grubby hands on my hips, I shoved the blade upward through his ribs and into his heart.

His lustful gaze fell replaced with shock, anger, and then nothing. He fell to the ground with a hard thud. Bending down, I wiped the blade off on his clothing and then sat on the edge of the bed waiting for my suitors to come.

After a few minutes, I got tired of waiting. I went to the bathroom and wiped off the blood that had splattered on me from the assassin. Then I grabbed the sheet off the bed and threw it over the guy. Dead bodies didn't really bother me but being around it this long was starting to freak me out. At least, with a sheet over it, I didn't have to look at it.

With nothing left to do, I chewed on my thumb. Where the hell were they? It couldn't take that long to interrogate someone. Surely the assassin had been noticed by someone.

Just as I was about to get up to grab a towel from the bathroom, so I could hunt someone down, the door burst open. All three of my suitors came rushing in their weapons at ready.

Snorting, I hopped off the bed and kicked the body toward them. "Took you long enough."

A rush of questions came at me too fast for me to decipher who was asking what.

"Are you okay?"

"Why didn't you call for help?"

"Who is he?"

Firestar was the first to reach me, his hands skimming over my still nude form looking for any kind of wound. Then he leveled me with a serious stare. "Did he touch you?"

I simpered up at him. "Only long enough for me to kill him."

"I apologize," Jack said, coming to stand beside me. "I don't understand. Last time, you were so scared, and we hadn't even encountered the assassin but this time..."

I frowned at his assessment. I had been scared before, but for some reason, this time fear hadn't even registered. I had only been thinking about staying alive.

"Either way," Raiden interrupted not waiting for me to answer. "I'm glad he's dead and not you." Kicking him over with his foot, he squatted down and searched his body. When he found nothing, his eyes looked to me. "Did he say who hired him?"

My lips twisted into an unpleasant grimace. "Ned."

"Ned?" Raiden asked, and then his face hardened. "As in your cousin, Ned? The one who had already tried to hurt you once before?"

I nodded solemnly. "Seems my cousin didn't want to wait for my father to dispatch me and decided to do it himself."

"And through someone else, so he wouldn't be blamed for it," Firestar added before pulling his shirt over his head and handing it to me. When I gave him a questioning look, he said, "You're distracting."

Giving him a coy grin, I slid the shirt over my head and let it settle over my thighs. The tension in the room lowered slightly now that I was concealed but not completely.

"What now?" I asked, more than ready to be out of my room now that it had to be cleaned again.

The three of them exchanged a look before Raiden came over to me, taking my hands in his own. "We found out who the raiders were working for."

The way they were acting made me uneasy. Why weren't they just telling me? Why all the dramatics?

"Well, who is it then?" I cocked an expectant brow at them.

"Maya," Raiden softly said, his hand cupping my face. "It was your father."

16

———

Like with Ned, I wished I felt surprised. But when Raiden told me the raiders worked for my father, I felt nothing. Just disappointed I hadn't figured it out sooner.

I briefly wondered if my mother knew. Then dismissed the idea. Of course, she didn't. She'd never approve of such meaningless destruction. Both she and my sister had wanted me to help end the raids. If anything, my mother knew something was happening but not to what extent.

Just more to add to my plate of things to worry about. As if I didn't have enough on it already. Getting pregnant was hard work, let alone trying to do it and stop war from breaking out in Waesigar. No one wanted that to happen, least of all me.

"How do you know?" I asked after a moment, my eyes on the dead body on the ground. Eventually, we would have to call someone to take it away, but when they did, we wouldn't have any privacy for a little while. There'd be questions and worse yet suspicions. It also meant Lady Nariko would be even more adamant about using me. This time though I might not be offered compensation.

"The men wouldn't talk," Firestar said and the tone he used told me everything. They had resorted to torture. I shuddered at the thought. Torture was something I'd never had the stomach for, nor had my father for that matter. It was the only thing we really had in common besides our blood. It was ironic that his own men couldn't handle it either.

"But they eventually talked," Raiden added, a pensive look on his face. "They didn't give us many details before we left them to my brothers, but they did say they were paid by the Western Lord."

Chewing on my bottom lip, I rolled around what they said in my mind. My father had always been a power-hungry man. He craved control over everything else. Sometimes, well most of the time, even above his own family. I wasn't back in Waesigar for nothing. He'd have never brought me back unless it benefited him. God forbid it was because he missed me. I thought I'd never meet anyone as bad as him until I'd met Raiden's mother. Boy had I been wrong.

I hadn't been kidding when I said he and Lady Nariko would have been a perfectly deadly match. Though they were likely to kill the other just so they wouldn't have to share power. My father was as suspicious as he was greedy for power. I felt bad for Raiden's father being saddled with such a woman. I had a feeling Lord Shen was still around because he let her call the shots.

"Did they say why?" I half-wished they hadn't, I didn't think I could take any more news today or this century. I'd only just taken a nap, but the stress of the day had me wanting to curl back into bed once more.

Raiden didn't seem happy to be talking about it. Probably because he had such a good relationship with his own family. Nevertheless, he shrugged and admitted, "As far as we can tell, they were just told to cause chaos in the realms. That's why there was such a mixture of dragons. He'd recruited from the unaligned. Who, as you know, are more than happy to stick it to their former lords." He gave me a sour look.

Jack made a sound of agreement. "I hardly

blamed them." When Firestar and I just stared at him, he quickly added, "No offense meant, but your father is power hungry and yours is a thief. Hardly men to rally behind."

I couldn't argue with him. Besides Raiden's mother, his family was pretty normal. Jack on the other hand. I didn't know much about Jack's family. He didn't talk about them much or at all. I had no idea how he felt about my father's actions regarding Waesigar or me. Jack had always kept his thoughts and opinions close to his chest, but in this instance, I'd have liked him to voice his worries to the group, or me at least.

Either way, no matter what any of them thought, I knew that it was only a matter of time before they came for us. Or rather me. But since they were mated to me, they might very well be seen as guilty by association. For once, I wished I hadn't slept with all of them. Then at least some of them might be able to get away without being brought down with me.

Damned father.

"So, how long do we have?" I asked.

"I don't understand what you are asking." Jack glanced from me to the others with a curious raise of his brows. "How long do we have until they come for the body?"

"She means," Firestar stepped in, placing an arm around my waist. "How long until your family," he pointed a finger at Raiden with a bit of an accusatory glint in his eyes. "Start coming to us with questions and threats."

"No, no." Raiden shook his head, disbelief in his voice. "My family wouldn't do that, and besides I already told my brothers Maya had nothing to do with this. She'd only been back for a few months, and these raids started way before that."

I snorted. The poor guy, I want to feel bad for him, but at this point, he was just being naïve. "Do you really think they won't take advantage of having the heir of the Western lands in their home? Especially, when they just found out its lord was now their enemy?"

Raiden didn't answer which wasn't good. He'd been so sure his family was right and good, but now he wasn't so sure. Then again, his mother was a right beast, and he'd never even noticed, so it was hardly surprising.

"We shouldn't jump to conclusions." Jack moved away from the group and shifted toward the door. "Let us find out ourselves their intentions before making enemies where there are none. Besides, everyone in the kingdom knows you bear no love for your father."

"Or him for me, it seems," I muttered mostly to myself. Not that it was news to me. Once you banish your child for no reason other than to keep the line of succession in your control you kind of lose all hope that your father cared for you.

"I agree with Jack." Raiden strode across the room to stand by the ice dragon. "We should talk to my father and brothers. Find out what else they learned before we are making any kind of decisions."

I stared at them both not wanting to be the downer of the group but knowing they didn't know what I knew. What was worse was I still hadn't told Raiden about his mother's proposal and adding it to the possibility that I might now be a prisoner of war? I didn't see it helping our relationship any.

"Very well," I sighed reluctantly and then turned to Firestar. "Will you stay and help me find something suitable to wear? It seems I have yet to get any new clothing."

"Sure." Firestar nodded at Jack and Raiden. Then when they had left, and we were alone, he asked, "What did you want to talk about?"

Brow raised, I asked, "How do you know I wanted to talk about anything? I really need more clothes."

Firestar snorted. "We might have been apart for five years, but I know you well enough to know you wouldn't agree to wait and see. So, what is it?"

Rather than beat around the bush, I blurted out, "Lady Nariko wants me to screw her sons for power and has threatened to leak the information to everyone in the kingdom if I don't do it."

Waiting for Firestar to explode, I was sadly disappointed when he only laughed. Shifting my weight, I shoved at the massive man, though he barely moved. "It's not funny. She knows about your father needing money and has offered to fairly compensate us for my services," I mockingly mimicked her words and then scoffed. "I'm not a high-class hooker she can just buy when she wants to and who's to know if it would stop at her sons. Why not her whole army?" I waved my arms in the air, paying no mind that I was ranting. "Or her husband?"

Firestar, the smart man that he was, waited until I was done before trying to speak. "I can't say I'm shocked. To be honest, I'm surprised it's taken anyone this long for her to try. My men weren't exactly known for keeping secrets."

"They kept yours well enough," I pointed out with a sneer.

"Well, that was when it was for the good of the kingdom." He drew me into his arms and while I didn't return his embrace, I didn't fight it. "When I put you above that they turned on me easily. You saw it yourself."

"Yes, well," I grumbled, leaning into his embrace. "I could hardly fault them but the mother of my own lover? That I can't forgive. Let alone the fact that she threatened me to do it. Like I'm just going to lay back and take it with her holding that over my head."

"Do Raijin and Fujin know?" Firestar asked, placing his chin on top of my head.

"No," I answered, shaking my head slightly. "She hasn't told them yet. I have the feeling she wants me to make it all my idea, so they will think I want to mate with them."

"Fucking and mating are not the same thing," Firestar growled, the sound rumbling through my entire being making my dragoness stir.

"I know, but I have a hard time seeing them not

taking it that way. Especially, if they think Raiden is all right with it."

"Which he wouldn't be," Firestar quickly interjected. "He might be easy going on most things, but when it comes to you, he's fiercely protective. Do you remember how he reacted when you added me to your bed? I don't see him wanting his brothers anywhere near what belongs to him. Well, us."

Firestar stating I belonged to them should have bothered me, but it only made me proud that they didn't have an issue sharing me. Belonging to not one but three different men was strange. Most women would be happy to find just one person to be with, and I had three. Wasn't fair, really. My friend Bianca on Earth would have had a field day if I told her about them, let alone that they thought I belonged to them.

Feminism and such. Though, I didn't see it that way. They belonged to me as much as I did them. None of us were trying to hinder the other from doing what they wanted. It wasn't like I was chained to them. No, it was more like the partnership I always wanted. Sure, we made mistakes. My blunder today with Jack and the blade was one example. I didn't expect it to be the last one either.

"Should I tell Raiden?" I asked finally, pulling

away from Firestar. "I mean how do I tell Raiden? This will devastate him."

Firestar pressed his lips together in a thin line before making a derisive sound. "I think you must handle this on your own, and then afterward, when it is all said and done, you tell Raiden. Remember we still don't know how they will react to the news of your father's attacks. No need to add more fuel to the fire."

I let out an exasperated breath. "This is getting so ridiculous. Sometimes I wish I'd have stayed on Earth. Told Ned and my father to go fuck themselves."

"You still can, and in fact, I encourage it." Firestar ushered me across the room and out into the hallway where he pointed us toward his room. "Both of those men have done nothing but bring misery to you. Ned more recently but your father…" Firestar shook his head in disgust as he opened the door to his bedroom. "Your father is a piece of work, a category of evil all on his own."

I should have defended my father. That would be what the dutiful daughter would do, but really Firestar was right, and I couldn't fault him for saying something I had thought myself.

Firestar left me in the middle of his room while

he went over to his dresser. He pulled open the bottom drawer and withdrew a gray pair of cotton pants. Handing them to me, I started to say they wouldn't fit me until I saw the drawstrings at the waist.

Shoving one leg and then the other into the sweatpants, I tried to figure out the best way to tell Lady Nariko where she could shove her offer. I had to be tactful and polite. If I told her what I really thought, she might very well throw me in her dungeon with the rest of the raiders. At least, the ones who hadn't already died from inter-rogation.

A faint knock on a door in the hallway made Firestar and I move back toward the door. Opening it up, we ducked our heads out to see the teenager who had taken me to tea with Lady Nariko. Which only meant he was here for one thing.

"Hello," I called out, making the boy jump in place. Spinning around, his eyes widened as he took in Firestar's looming form.

"Uh, I..." the teen shuffled his feet and stared at Firestar.

Firestar, the darling, crossed his arms and puffed his chest out in warning. I tried to keep the smile off my face, but his act was too silly to go along with.

The boy dropped his gaze to the floor and took a deep breath in before approaching us.

"My lady..." he started but then peeked up to look at Firestar who only seemed more menacing by the minute. The teen's mouth gaped open, and I swore he would have rather swallowed his tongue than talk to us. Poor boy.

Smacking Firestar on the arm, I said, "Leave the boy alone. Let him do his job." The teen seemed to relax a bit as I stepped in front of Firestar as a bit of a barrier between them but not much.

Clearly still afraid of Firestar, the teen shook in his boots before he cleared his throat and started again. "My lady wishes..." I had to give it to him though, he was dedicated to his work because he stuttered out, "Lady Nariko requests your presence."

Exchanging a look with Firestar, I waved the boy to lead the way. It looked like my time was up. Lady Nariko wanted her answer, and she wanted it now. I only hoped her husband hadn't gotten wind of her request now that my father's plot in this had been discovered.

17

As I followed my guide toward where I was going to meet Lady Nariko, I couldn't help but feel like I was walking to my doom. I knew what was going to happen. Or rather I could guess.

Lady Nariko would be annoyingly smug about the whole thing, and when I told her no, she'd threaten me. Which made having Firestar there to back me up all the better. She'd have a hard time intimidating me with him at my side. He'd already proven that with the servant boy leading us.

When the teen stopped at Lady Nariko's door, he tried to take off on me once again, but I stopped him with my hand. "What's your name?"

He glanced up at me shyly before his eyes

darted to Firestar. Swallowing visibly, he muttered, "Jinn, my lady."

Smiling down at him, I offered him my hand which he took hesitantly before dropping his arm as if afraid Firestar would lop it off. "All right, Jinn, thank you for bringing us here. Could you do me a favor?"

"Of course, my lady." He nodded his head up and down like one of those bobbleheads I'd seen in Ryan's car.

"Could you find Prince Raiden," I said. "Tell him I need him at his mother's rooms. Tell him it's important."

"Of course, my lady," he said once more and gave me a slight bow. His eyes darted to Firestar for a brief second before he hurried away.

"Are you expecting trouble?" Firestar asked after Jinn was out of sight. I didn't even bother chastising him about messing with the boy all the way here, my nerves were already focused on what was to come.

"If you'd been with her the last time I was here, then you would too." I sighed and adjusted my borrowed sweatpants. "She might pretend to be a nice old lady who loves her sons to the public, but in reality, she's a mean old bitch."

Firestar snorted. "She's not that good of an actor."

He was right she wasn't. How she had fooled her family for so long bewildered me. An idiot could see through her backhanded compliments and thinly veiled threats. But then again love made everyone stupid. Especially, family.

"Nevertheless, don't expect this to be pleasant. She wants me to give her sons powers too so she will try anything to get me to say yes. Which means she's going to let her bitch flag fly once she realizes I'm saying no." I knocked on the door and waited for the voice from inside to tell me to enter.

When Lady Nariko saw Firestar, her brows rose, but she didn't immediately demand he leave. Instead, she glanced at her table with a frown. "I apologize, but I wasn't expecting two guests. I'm afraid I don't have enough cups for tea."

Firestar didn't even respond to her like it would have been appropriate for him to do. Instead, his attention was purely focused on the corners of the balcony. What was he looking at? Turning toward where he was glaring, I could barely make out the form of a few figures hiding in the shadows.

Did she expect a fight? I hadn't come offering

violence, but I wasn't completely surprised she would think of it.

Noticing our attention was not on her, Lady Nariko waved a hand. "Oh, don't mind them. They are only here because of the prisoners in the palace. Can't have the Lady of the East being taken by traitors." Her eyes locked on me in a clear warning. Like I cared about hurting her, I just wanted to get away from her and her other sons.

"Understandable," I said, nodding before taking a seat opposite of her.

"Tea?" she offered, holding the pot over my cup.

I nodded and offered my cup up. "Thank you."

We sat there in silence for a moment with Firestar standing over us. The tension in the air was plausible, and I wondered when she would ask for my answer. However, her full focus wasn't on me but Firestar who had stayed standing close enough to make it uncomfortable.

"Please sit down or go over there. Something," Lady Nariko huffed and shook her head. "Really, men can be so overprotective. I don't know how you handle three all the time. They're more hormonal than we are half the time."

I nodded politely and shot Firestar a look.

Glancing to the side, I gestured for him to go a few feet over next to a couch. That would keep Firestar between whomever was waiting on the balcony, and I didn't want him to be any further away from me than he had to be.

When Firestar was settled, I decided to break the ice by apologizing. "I'm sorry for my appearance. I haven't had a chance to find more clothes, and after the battle, my last outfit was soaked."

"Oh, dear." Lady Nariko covered her mouth in mock horror. "Why didn't you say something sooner? I can have a whole wardrobe brought to your room within the hour."

"Thank you," I said, picking up the teacup in front of me. "That's so kind of you."

"It's nothing for the future mother of my first grandchildren." Lady Nariko faked a humble bow of her head. If I didn't know the beast within waiting to strike out at any moment, I'd have been fooled. I covered my eye roll by taking a sip from my cup.

"Well, he could be the father or Jack or Firestar. Really any of them, they all have an equal chance at being the father." I couldn't help but point out with a smile at the fire dragon. He nodded his head but didn't comment though there was a twinkle in his eye that said he approved.

"Of course, of course," Lady Nariko agreed, nodding as well, though there were tight lines around her mouth. How did she keep herself in check so easily? I'd have blown my top by now if I'd been in her position. Which was probably why she had been able to fool her family for so long. Years and years of practice and deceit.

That was the first hint that something was wrong. She had been far too agreeable. Too nice. Either she thought I was coming to tell her yes, which I had given her no indication that I would, or she knew something I didn't.

"Speaking of fathering children." The Lady of the East sat her cup down and laced her fingers over her stomach. "I hope you have had time to think about my offer. Seeing you have brought your lover with you, I assume he knows of our arrangement." She turned her cold gaze on Firestar who didn't so much as flinch under its gaze.

"Yes, Firestar is aware of what you want from me." I shifted in my seat the very thought of it made me uneasy. "We have talked about it at length, and I believe I have come to a decision."

Lady Nariko's lips curled into a self-satisfied grin. "Oh, have you, I do hope it is good n—"

"No," I cut her off before she could praise herself on her cleverness. I took great joy in watching the smug look on her face morph into confusion. Better than straight anger I supposed.

"No?" She cocked her ear toward me as if to hear me better. "What do you mean no?"

Sitting back in my seat, I took another sip from my cup and then grinned. "You know exactly what I mean. I will not now, or ever let you use me like that."

Lady Nariko offered me a pitying look. "Oh, my dear, I had no intention of making you feel used. You are being paid for your services after all." She turned her all-knowing eyes to Firestar. "She did tell you about my offer, didn't she? I'll pay all your father's debts if she does this one thing for me."

Firestar stood abruptly, causing Lady Nariko to move back in her seat. A smile tipped my lips at her fear. Good. She should fear him. If she knew what was good for her, anyway.

"Lady Nariko," Firestar's deep voice reverberated through the room and even the men on the balcony tensed. "My upbringing requires me to treat you with respect, but since you have none for those around you nor the woman your son loves, I have none for you."

"Why I never..." Lady Nariko cried out and tried to argue back, but Firestar cut her off.

"Furthermore, only the lowest of beings would use someone like an object to further their own powers the way you want Maya to do. If you weren't the Lady of the East, and my friend's mother, I'd kill you right now." His eyes shot to the guards who had moved closer to us. "As it stands, I don't believe in unnecessary bloodshed and only ask that you accept Maya's answer and never speak of it again."

Lady Nariko didn't say anything for a moment, and I thought maybe Firestar had gotten through to her. An optimistic thought, sure, but it wiggled its way into my mind, anyway. So, when the Lady of the East shoved her chair back her face full of rage, I had to say I was surprised.

"You don't know who you are talking to," she snarled at Firestar like a mother cub protecting her young. "I could have your tongue cut out just for speaking to me that way."

"Then do it and let us be done with this conversation," Firestar countered, half bowing to her in a taunting manner.

When she seemed to realize that Firestar would not back down, she turned her rage on me. "Control your mate at once, or I will have both of you arrested for treason."

"How?" I angled my head to the side with a curious raise of my brows. "How is our refusal treason? In fact, neither of us are citizens of your kingdom so anything we did wouldn't be considered treason."

"Then you are declaring war on the East," she shot back, baring her teeth at me, her eyes glowing yellow as she lost control of her dragon.

"I've done no such thing," I countered, standing. I sat my cup back down on the table and took my place by Firestar's side. "You offered me a choice. Help your sons gain the powers that my men have in exchange for money, and my secrets kept or…"

"I'll throw you to the wolves," she cut me off with a growl. "And believe me, you will find far less pleasant offers to get between those legs than what I have offered. Think wisely on your next words."

I wished I had half the balls that Lady Nariko had, but when I thought about what I would be giving up to be as brazen as her, I couldn't accept it. I'd rather keep my soul intact. Sadly, the more I spoke to Lady Nariko, the less I understood how she could have produced such wonderful children. Then again, my father was at least as ruthless as Lady Nariko and look what he'd done to me.

"Very well," I said and took a deep breath as I locked my eyes with hers. "Tell my secrets if you must. I don't care. I will not now or ever fuck your sons just because you can't be happy with what you have." She tried to interrupt me, but I put my hand up. "And if you ever hope to see any of the grand-children produced by Raiden and me, I would come to terms with my decision. Or mark my words, he will find out what kind of woman you truly are."

"Don't threaten me, girl." Lady Nariko hissed, seeming not to get the point.

"Oh, it's not a threat, it's a promise." I stepped toward her, making her take one back. "And I promise your sons will never forgive you for what you have done here. Raiden especially. You will be lucky if he ever speaks to you again. Believe me, I know how it feels to realize one of your family doesn't love you anymore. It never goes away. Ever."

Lady Nariko's gaze wavered slightly, and I thought maybe, just maybe I had gotten through to her. That was until she straightened her spine and seemed to regain her composure.

"Guards," she commanded, and four armed dragons stepped out from the shadows. Instantly, Firestar and I went on the defensive though they hadn't offered violence. Yet. "Arrest them."

The guards closed in on us, the swords at their waist slightly drawn. Not threatening but ready for us to resist.

Firestar's fire formed into his kusarigamas in an instant. I only had the dagger Jack had given me, but it was back in the room where I'd stupidly left it.

My eyes locked with Lady Nariko, and I growled, "You don't want to do this."

Her lips curled into a wicked grin. "Oh, my dear child, you have no idea how much I do. Please attack, it will be so much easier to convince my husband you are in line with your father. Then you will never see my Raiden again. Though, I will be sure to have my other sons visit you and perhaps a guard or two." Her eyes flickered to the men surrounding us. "Can't let someone with your abilities go to waste after all. Enemy of the kingdom or not."

She inclined her head slightly, and the guards began to close in on us. My blood pounded in my ears as I realized there was no way out of this one. Firestar could probably take them out but how would we explain it to Lord Shen? Lady Nariko had him and her sons wrapped around her finger. What was our word against hers?

Firestar readied his kusarigamas preparing to lash out at the nearest guard, but before he could, the doors to Lady Nariko's rooms swung open. Relief filled me as Jack, Raiden, and his brothers came barging through. Jack and Raiden took one look at the guards threatening us before they too unleashed their weapons.

At least, I knew they were on my side. Not that there was any question about Jack, but Raiden was a bit touch and go. Though the way his eyes lit with anger and a growl rumbled from his mouth, I knew a hundred percent that no matter what his mother said, he would be on my side.

18

"Mother, what is the meaning of this?" Raijin cried out before a battle could start in the middle of the sitting room.

"What does it look like, dears?" She gestured to Firestar and me with a grin. "I'm apprehending criminals."

"What makes you think Maya and Firestar are criminals?" Raiden snarled, anger lighting his eyes yellow. "They've done nothing wrong."

"Oh?" Lady Nariko quirked a brow. "If that was so, why did they come in here intent on assassinating me if they weren't part of Lord Dannan's plan?"

Raijin and Fujin glanced at us and then at each other clearly unsure who to believe. Raiden, on the other hand, didn't even so much flinch at his mother's words of accusation. Good news for us, but with his brothers on the fence, it could potentially mean bad news.

"Maya," Raiden said slowly, his eyes never leaving his mother's victorious expression. "Explain."

I opened my mouth to tell him exactly what was happening here, but his mother cut me off. "No need, dear. I've already told you. I invited dear Maya to tea as I had done before, but when she came, she brought this brute with her." She gestured violently at Firestar with an angry frown. "Then she proceeded to threaten my life. Of course, I'm lucky your father had posted guards on the balcony to keep me safe, or you might be burying me."

"Still could," I muttered to myself, earning me a glare from Lady Nariko.

"See, right there. She threatened me."

Sighing, I held my hands up to show I had no weapons as I turned around to face Raiden. "Yes, I threatened her just now with you in the room, only because she is being ridiculous and nasty as she has been the entire time I've been here."

Raiden and his brothers' brows furrowed as if the very thought of their mother being that way was incomprehensible, and to them, it probably was. They had spent their whole lives believing their mother was good and just, and here I was throwing a metaphorical wrench into their beliefs.

Thankfully, the brothers were not as rash as they appeared and stood down. Waving a hand at me, Fujin said, "Go ahead then. Tell us what exactly happened here."

I glanced at Lady Nariko and asked, "Do you want to tell them, or should I? This is your last chance. I told you I didn't want to destroy your relationship with them, but if you don't do this, I will."

Lady Nariko hissed at me and stubbornly remained silent. With a sad sigh, I turned back to the brothers. This was not going to be easy.

"Fujin, Raijin," I addressed the twins with a solemn expression. "You were right to wonder how Raiden and the others had gained such awesome powers."

"Yes," Fujin answered with a grin. "We hope to one day train hard enough to have some of our own." He bumped arms with his twin who returned his smile so happy at the prospect of becoming more powerful. I really hated to burst their bubble.

"Well, you won't. Not ever," I said, causing lightning princes' faces to sober. "At least, I don't think so. I don't know how it works exactly." I chanced a glance at Raiden whose face had begun to harden as he realized where I was going with this.

"What do you mean?" Raijin asked, taking a step forward, which only made Firestar shift closer to me. His eyes darted to Firestar, and he stopped his progression.

"I mean," I continued, pushing Firestar away some so I could see their faces. "That your brother, along with my other suitors, gained powers they would normally need centuries of experience to obtain within moments of laying with me."

The room went silent as the brothers seemed to roll around what I had said. The guards still stood at ready for their lord and lady's command while Raiden and Jack looked like they had swallowed something foul. None of us wanted to be in this position right now. Our secret was out, and there was nothing I could do about it. I just hoped we could keep it in this room. If we couldn't, I didn't know what would happen.

"So," Fujin finally said slowly. "You are saying." He paused his eyes darting to his little brother and then back to me. "That you have some kind of magic power giver down there?"

I shrugged a shoulder, a lifted a brow. "Yes?"

"Aww, man." Fujin smacked Raiden on the arm. "You lucky bastard. Father originally wanted me to go to mate the Western Lord's daughter, and I had to convince him to send you instead. Now, I wished I'd accepted." He shook his head with a big grin on his face. Surprisingly, there was no envy there, just humor at what he'd missed out on.

"Yes," Raiden answered his eyes locked on mine. "I'm one lucky guy." I shivered at the intensity of his gaze, feeling like he could read my mind. Which I wished meant I didn't have to say it at all, but I knew I had to or it would never be real, not truly.

"So, what does this all have to do with our mother?" Raijin asked, not letting the main point of the conversation get shoved under Fujin's jokes.

I shot a look back at Lady Nariko, giving her one more chance to come clean, but she crossed her arms over her chest and stuck her nose in the air. Very well. Here it goes.

"Your mother figured out my little condition," I explained using my hands to illustrate my point. "And well..." I trailed off and tried to find a nice way of putting it but couldn't find one.

Firestar, on the other hand, didn't care about being nice about it and simply blurted out, "She threatened Maya. She said that if she didn't fuck you both and give you the same kind of powers, well…" He gestured at the guards.

The room went dead silent. I swore I could barely hear anyone breathing. Had the news been that bad? One look at Raiden's face, and I knew it hadn't only been bad but worse.

All at once, the room burst into chaos. All three brothers argued over the other, their words lost in a mix I couldn't figure out. They came toward us outrage clear on their faces. Firestar stepped between them and me, but it wasn't me they were after, it was their mother.

"How could you do this?" Raiden cried out, being the first one to get past me and to his mother's side. "She's not some toy you can just borrow and give back when you're done."

"I didn't say she was," Lady Nariko argued and tried to place her hands on Raiden, but he wouldn't let her touch him. "You don't understand. When you rule, you'll realize what it means to sacrifice everything for your kingdom."

"So, Maya is a sacrifice?" Raiden snarled, his hands glowing with magic as his temper raged out of control.

"I have to agree with Raiden, mother." Fujin stopped beside him with a nod. "That's low even for you."

So, they did know some of how their mother was, that was a small blessing. A huge weight lifted off me at the news. I didn't want to be the soul destruction of Lady Nariko's motherly image. Though, my stomach still rolled with mixed feelings. I wanted to leave them to hash it out, but I couldn't leave Raiden alone now. Not when he could need me.

"Not sacrifice really," Lady Nariko tried to change her words, but she had already damned herself. "And it's not like it would have been such a burden for her to have two more handsome men in her bed. I even offered to pay her!"

Raiden scoffed and took a step away from her.

"That's even worse. Now, she's not just a stepping stone to give our family power but a prostitute? Have you no shame?"

"And another thing," Raijin added, his own face filled with disgust. "We can find our own mates. We aren't your little boys anymore. We'll be lord of the Eastern lands soon enough."

"Not if you don't stop fighting you won't be," Lady Nariko growled her eyes hot. "You two act like children fighting over your favorite toy rather than two grown adults getting ready to take the throne. How am I supposed to know you can handle it if you can't even agree on anything?"

"Well, you are in luck, mother." Fujin gave her a callous grin. "We agree on one thing. You're under house arrest."

"What?" Her eyes widened as she tried to plead with her sons. "You can't do this, I'm your mother. I was only doing what I did out of love for you."

"For power you mean," Raijin sneered and gestured to the guards. "You stay with her until we get father here to decide what to do with her."

The guards glanced at the lords and then back to Lady Nariko as if unsure whose orders to follow. Fujin snapped his fingers drawing their attention back to him.

"We are your future Lords. You will obey us or be put in the dungeons with rest of the traitors." The guards didn't have to be told twice as they ushered Lady Nariko out of the sitting room and into her bedroom. I could still hear her wailing through the bedroom door.

I didn't have to wonder what would happen next because Raiden took one look at me and strode out of the room. My eyes brimmed with unshed tears at the hurt in his gaze before he left. It might not have been my fault, but part of him blamed me for it. It was clear as day on his face.

"Give him time, Maya," Fujin said, placing a comforting hand on my shoulder. "He always held her up on a pedestal."

"He's her baby," Raijin confirmed with a sad shake of his head. "She's always been so careful around him. More so than us. We knew she was behind some of the dastardly things that have happened in the past, but we never expected anything like this." His gaze settled on me with a shameful frown. "I cannot apologize enough for the distress our mother has caused you and hope you will not blame her sons for their parent's mistakes."

"Of course not," I quickly said, shaking my head as the tears ran freely down my face. "I'd never imagine doing such a thing. I just feel so bad that I had to be the reason your picture of her was ruined."

"She did that all on her own." Jack stepped up beside me, wrapping an arm around me and pulling me near. I buried my face in his chest, his cool temperature felt good against my heated face. "Do not blame yourself for this at all."

"Raiden does though," I muttered into his embrace. "He hates me."

Firestar snorted. "You have that man wrapped around your little finger. He could no more hate you than any of the rest of us. If anything, he's upset because his mother hurt you. Not the other way around."

"Do you think so?" I picked my head up and glanced at Firestar and the brothers who nodded solemnly.

I wanted to believe them. I knew logically it wasn't my fault. I hadn't made his mother do those things. Hell, I'd even warned her what it would cost her, but she did it anyway. Then again, I wasn't a mother, I didn't know how far I would go for my offspring. Maybe being a parent made you a bit crazy.

It would sure explain my father's problem.

Sadly, that didn't change the aftermath. Raiden had finally seen what his mother was like. It was what I wanted, but even so, it also had hurt him. I could only pray now that it wouldn't ruin the strenuous relationship we already had.

19

I didn't dare sleep by myself that night. In fact, we should have left right away, but Raiden insisted we wait and say goodbye properly in the morning when our heads were cooler.

Curled up to Raiden, who had also insisted I stay with him, I couldn't sleep. Though, he had wanted me to stay Raiden hadn't done much more than grunt at me from the moment I came to his room. I didn't know what to do. My mind reeled with what had happened. I felt so bad that Raiden and his brothers had finally seen how nasty their mother truly was, and I knew if I felt this horrible, Raiden probably felt worse.

"Raiden," I murmured quietly, in case he was sleeping. "Are you awake?"

"Hmm?" was Raiden's response, not telling me if he was actually sleeping. Shifting on the bed, I leaned up on my elbow to get a good look at his face. Before I could sit up completely, Raiden's hand stopped me. "Don't, Maya."

Sighing, I drew my hand along Raiden's chest, my fingers running through his chest hair. "We should talk about what happened."

"No, we shouldn't."

I could hear the exhaustion in his voice, and I couldn't deny I felt the same. Nevertheless, letting something like this fester would not only hurt our relationship but destroy it all together. The humans always say that communication is the number one reason relationships fail. Well, I didn't know if any of those humans had ever met a dragon shifter male, but they weren't exactly the talkative type. Not unless it was about fighting or fucking.

"Raiden," I tried again determined not to let our relationship go to the dumps because of this. "I'm sorry about your mother."

"Thank you."

Frowning at his short answer, I wondered if he was still angry at me for not telling him. I knew I'd be mad if my family had gone behind my back and propositioned one of my men. Though, I also didn't have false images of my family. Or rather my father. He wouldn't even do it behind my back. So confident in his own decisions, he'd do it right in front of me—without consulting me.

"I should have told you right away," I continued with an apologetic sigh. "I just didn't want you to get hurt. I know how much you love your mother."

Raiden didn't answer for a long time, and I thought he might have fallen asleep on me. Then when he did speak, I wished he had been sleeping.

"I'm not stupid," Raiden snapped, shifting in the bed to face me.

My eyes locked on his darkened face, I shook my head. "I never thought you were. Just..." I winced wishing I felt differently, "A bit blind."

"I know my mother has a temper and can be a bit overambitious," he explained, defending her like any son would. Still, I couldn't let it go.

"I think prostituting out your mate is a bit more than ambitious," I pointed out with a disgusted twist of my lips.

"You're right," Raiden answered, his hand coming out to stroke my face. "What she did was unacceptable and unforgivable. How I could be so blind to how she really is, I don't know." I felt him shake his head beside me before rolling back onto his back. "I still love her. She's my mother."

"Of course, you do." I curled up to him again, so that I could still see his face. "I wouldn't expect you to suddenly stop caring about her."

"I just can't understand how she could be so heartless." Raiden sat up suddenly, making me roll to the side. He hunched over his legs his back turned to me. "What kind of person thinks it's okay to use someone like that? Not even the fact that you are mine."

"It's a good thing I am then." I placed my hand on his shoulder, making him turn to me.

"Are what?"

"Yours," I murmured, ducking my head down.

"How do you do it?" Raiden asked, tipping my chin back up. "You have three men who adore you and, yet you never treat any of us less than the other."

Flushing, I was happy he couldn't see my embarrassment. "I don't know. I never expected to be in this situation, let alone be happy about it. You each give me something different, and I couldn't bear to lose any of you."

"You won't," Raiden assured me. "At least, not

me. No matter what happens, I won't leave your side." He grabbed my hands in his and stroked the top of my hands. "I want you to know, I don't blame you for my mother's actions. I'm sorry if it seemed like I did."

"I know but thank you for saying so." I put my hand on top of his and then leaned forward to press my lips to his.

He didn't respond at first, and I wondered if we would ever get back to normal. Then like a fire had been stoked within him, his hands came up to cup my face, angling it to the side as he kissed me back. His tongue attacked my mouth as if he were claiming every inch of it.

My palms found the hard planes of his chest as we laid back down, Raiden between my thighs. It didn't take much foreplay to get us ready and when Raiden slid inside of me, it was just right. Kissing and touching, we couldn't get enough of each other as we moved together as one.

When we came down from our high, I realized something.

"You know," I said, tracing the lines of his chest with my fingertips. "I think that's the first time we ever just had plain old vanilla sex, no kink."

"Oh?" Raiden commented his tone that of a

completely sated man. Then without warning, he was above me again my hands pinned above my head. "I can fix that." His voice had taken on that commanding bass he always seemed to have when we made love, but there was something different about it. Something more vulnerable.

Laughing at his antics, I shifted beneath him until he released me. "I wasn't complaining, just making an observation."

"So, you like me with a little kink?" He rubbed his already hardened length against my hip.

Cupping his chin in my hand, I leaned up and pressed my lips to his with a soft kiss. "I love you any way I can have you."

Raiden went still against me, and I feared I had gone too far. Should I have waited to tell him? I hadn't exactly planned it, it'd just come out.

"You love me?" Raiden asked after what felt like an agonizing amount of time.

"Yes?" I drew out, cautious of how he would react. I didn't expect him to say it back, but I didn't think I could take it if he denied my feelings.

Raiden picked up my hand and laced my fingers with his own before bringing it to his mouth. "Good because I love you too."

"You do?" I cocked a brow before realizing he couldn't see me in the dark.

"Of course, I do. I love your kindness and spirit. And bravery," he chuckled. "Not everyone would go against my mother and live." He bopped me on the nose before his hand slid down my face to cup my breast. "I love touching you, knowing you are all mine." His hand then settled on my flat stomach. "And when you are fat with child, I will love you even more."

"Fat with child, you say?" I said dryly. "That's good to know."

"Just more of you to love," Raiden countered with a laugh. "I'm sure the others will think the exact same thing. You will be one adorable pregnant woman."

"More like one miserable one," I grumbled and then gasped as Raiden's fingers stroked between my thighs.

Before we could get intimate, there was a knock on the door. We glanced at each other though we couldn't see very well. Neither of us had been expecting visitors, which didn't bode well. Who would knock on our door this late?

"Stay here," Raiden commanded as he got out

of the bed. A flash of light filled the room as Raiden conjured his trident. The glow from it lit up the room so I could watch him walk across the room butt naked. I thought about reminding him but then shrugged and let him do his thing.

"Who is it?" Raiden asked his hand on the doorknob.

"It's us," Firestar's voice came through the door. "Let us in."

Raiden glanced at me and smirked before asking, "Us who?"

I could practically feel Firestar's irritation on the other side of the door and covered my mouth to keep myself from laughing.

"Jack and Firestar," the fire dragon growled from the hallway. "Now let us in before I break down the door."

"Okay, okay," Raiden said and opened the door. "Keep your britches on."

When the door was open, Firestar and Jack marched into the room. They didn't look happy. Even more so when they saw me in the bed.

"Get up," Firestar demanded and grabbed my clothes off the floor before tossing them to me. "And get dressed. We're leaving."

"Leaving?" I asked as I scurried out of bed and into my clothes. "Why?"

Jack pressed his lips together into a thin line before letting out a disgusted sound. "Change of plans."

"Why? What happened?" Raiden asked, pulling on his own clothes. "Was it my mother?"

"I overheard a guard talking about arresting some traitors in a few hours. Conspirators with the raiders," Firestar explained and then formed his kusarigamas in his hands, swinging them for good measure. "It's best if we are gone before then."

"Wait a minute." Raiden stepped between them his hands up in defense. "I have a hard time believing that my family would do that." We all shot him a look which made Raiden quickly add. "All right beside my mother, but I thought we had that all settled with my brothers earlier. How do you know they were talking about us?"

"Because," Firestar answered with a menacing growl. "They said that Western whore and her men. Know anyone else they could be talking about?" Firestar stared Raiden down and when he didn't answer, nodded. "Good, then let's go."

I helped Raiden gather up his belongings, and then we headed for the door. We were just ready to leave when another knock sounded. Glancing at each other, a sense of unease filling the room. Jack formed his war hammer, and I withdrew my dagger ready for an attack.

"Who is it?" Raiden asked, causing the others to glower at him. The smart thing would have been to open the door and attack before they knew we were even in there. Raiden might know how his family was now, but it didn't keep him from being too trusting.

"It's Raijin and Fujin," Raijin's voice answered. "We need to talk."

"About what?" Raiden asked for once not just opening the door to them. "We're sleeping."

"No, you aren't," Fujin argued. "We just saw the other two come in here. So, unless you are having foursome, open the damned door."

Raiden gave us a questioning look as if to ask what to do. Firestar tightened his grip on his weapons, his jaw clenching before nodding his consent. Breath held, I waited as Raiden opened the door for the second time in a span of a few minutes.

When the door swung open and revealed his brothers and only his brothers. We visibly relaxed.

We stepped back from the door, so they could come in and closed it tightly behind them.

Fujin and Raijin took in our drawn weapons and held their hands up, showing us, they were defenseless.

"Whoa there, we come in peace," Raijin said, dropping the bag in his hand. It fell to the ground with a loud clank, sounding heavier than it looked.

"What do you want?" Firestar asked, not dropping his weapons, though the brothers clearly weren't a threat.

"You need to leave," Fujin said, and when we stiffened added, "Don't get me wrong, you guys are always welcome by us, but mother..."

"Mother's a little bit more of a psycho than we thought," Raijin finished for him with an exasperated sigh. "She apparently didn't take our punishment as well as we hoped and escaped. She rallied her supporters, which—"

"Includes, some rich guy on the coast. Who, if the intel is right, has been just begging for a fight," Fujin interjected with a meaningful look to Raiden. "Which is why you need to leave now before they come for you."

"But we'll never get out of here without a fight," I said, looking to the others for confirmation.

"She's right," Raiden answered and then paused before asking, "Where's father?"

Fujin and Raijin glanced at each other and then Fujin said, "Dungeon. He was arrested shortly after we found out about mother."

"Then we must rescue him," Raiden cried out, heading for the door.

"No, Raiden." Fujin grabbed Raiden's arm, stopping him from leaving. "There's no time. We have to get out now."

"Fine," Raiden growled, not happy with the command. "Then the sooner we get out of here, the sooner we can come back and save him."

"Wait, what about you?" I asked the two brothers before we could leave them behind. "What if your mother comes for you?"

Raijin smirked. "Don't worry about us, we'll hold them off as long as we can so you can get away. We'll catch up with you."

Decision made, Fujin and Raijin took turns hugging Raiden, murmuring something to him I couldn't hear but chalked it up to brother stuff. They then turned to Jack and Firestar, clapping hands with them each with a respectful nod. When the time came for them to say goodbye to me, they're expression changed to distraught.

"We're so sorry, Maya," Fujin apologized and ran a hand through his hair, real anguish in his expression. "We would never have done what she wanted. Even if we thought you wanted to."

"Yeah," Raijin agreed with a quick nod. "We couldn't do that to Raiden or you. Not for all the powers in the world."

"Thanks, guys. That's really good to hear." I offered them a small smile to show them I didn't blame them for their mother's actions.

"Well, we know words can only go so far," Raijin continued, grabbing the bag that had been dropped to the ground. "So, we brought you a peace offering."

"This is a bottomless bag," Fujin explained shoving the dark purple bag at my feet. "It can carry all sorts of things, we even put a horse in there once." He chuckled and glanced at his brother with a smile.

I tried to pick up the bag expecting it to weigh a ton, but it was surprisingly light. Grinning up at the brothers, I hugged them both. "Thank you, it's a wonderful gift."

"We already packed it with everything you could need," Fujin continued, waving a hand at the bag. "Have you given any thought to where you will go next?"

I frowned at him and then looked at the guys. "Well, we can't go back to my home. My cousin wants me dead, and Firestar's father would be breathing down our necks to get the money we said we'd get him. So that leaves..."

"My home," Jack answered, coming forward. "We can go to the north. There are no raids there, the weather is too cold for anyone to try. And no one knows of you or your abilities," he finished with a soft expression.

"Are you sure?" I asked. It sounded too good to be true. "We could always find a portal and hide on Earth. Then come back when things have settled some. Or I've got a child to show them."

"Yes, I'm sure." Jack took the bag from me and placed a hand on my shoulder. "Besides, I would love to share my home with you. You've already seen these two's, it is only fair you spend time in mine."

"All right." I nodded before turning to the others. "It looks like we are heading north."

I didn't know if going north would solve our problems or only make them worse. I did know that it was better than the alternatives. We couldn't stay in Raiden's home while his mother was dead set on making me empower her sons. At my home, who knew what waited for me there. Ned might have fulfilled his promise to tattle to my father, or he could be biding his time waiting to kill me. Either way, going north was the only option. I just hoped it was the right one.

20

Leaving the room, we encountered our first set of guards. They took one look at our group before shouting for help.

"We've got this," Raijin said as he and Fujin readied their weapons and stood in front of us. "You go the other way. Raiden?"

"Yeah?"

"Be careful." Raijin gave him a meaningful look before charging at the guards.

Raiden took a step toward his brothers, but I grabbed his hand, forcing him to turn from the fight. "Come on, we'll see them again."

"Right." Raiden nodded before hurrying us down the hallway and out a side door. A spiral staircase laid before us, and we rushed down the stairs until we heard a commotion from the bottom. Pausing mid-step, we tried to turn to go back, but before we could, the shouts of the guards above filled my ears.

"We have to keep going," Firestar commanded, taking the lead, his kusarigamas clenched in his hands. "We'll have to fight our way through."

Running down the stairs, Firestar lashed out at the coming guards, knocking them back down the stairs and hopefully into the rest of the enemies. I held tightly to Raiden's hand as Jack brought up the rear. The sound of quickly approaching boots behind us made the ice dragon urge me forward.

"I don't want to accidentally hit you with this," he explained, holding his hammer in his hands.

I hurried away from Jack as he stayed behind to stop our incoming attackers. Firestar continued forward with Raiden and I close behind. The sound of fighting surrounded us, and magic filled the air. Blasts of flame leapt from Firestar's weapons as he smashed through two guards, reducing them to charred corpses in a split second. The smell of burned flesh hit my nose as Raiden pulled me past the bodies.

As Firestar reached the bottom, he stopped, waiting for us to catch up. The moment we neared

him, he cracked open the door leading to the courtyard, and when no one attacked him, peered
through the narrow opening.

"How's it looking?" I asked, handing Raiden
the bag his brother had given us. "Do you think we
can make it out?"

"Hard to tell, the king's men are fighting the
ones aligned with the queen, but I can't tell who's
fighting for whom." He sighed and shook his head.
"Our best chance is to try to get out unnoticed in
the shadows."

Nodding my head, I chewed on my thumb in
thought. I didn't expect it to be easy. We'd already
encountered so many men, I had a hard time
believing it would be easy enough to hide in the
shadows. Plus, the twins were fighting for us. I
didn't know them well, but I didn't want them to
die for us. It was bad enough Raiden's mother was
rebelling, but to lose his brothers too? I didn't know
how he would cope with it.

Feet pounding on the stairs made us tense, and
the guys shoved me behind them. Weapons at the
ready they prepared to attack whoever came at us,
but when Jack came around the spiral corner, we
relaxed a bit.

"Why are you waiting?" Jack asked, still coming

at us at a quick speed. "Let's go, there are more coming."

Not having to be told twice, Firestar pushed the door open and ushered us through.

The courtyard was a mess. Lightning dragon fought against lightning dragon, making the ground a dangerous place to be. Too focused on their own battles, we were able to get out the door and along the wall of the palace wall. Now we just had to find a way out of the palace and into the city. From there, maybe we could escape before anyone noticed.

"Maya," Raiden hissed at me, and I realized I had started to lag behind while lost in thought. Shaking my head, I quickened my footsteps to catch up with them all the while keeping an eye out around us. From the way it was looking, someone was losing, and I had a bad feeling it was us.

"Stop," Firestar commanded in a hushed tone.

We'd come to the corner of the wall and would now have to find a way out. We were only a few feet from being out in the open and out of the safety of the shadows. The gate even further away. I didn't see a way we were getting out without a fight.

"Raiden," Firestar said, grabbing the lightning dragon's attention. "Any ideas?"

Frowning, Raiden stroked his chin. "We can't fly over, they have dozens of men on the walls that'd shoot us down in a second." He became quiet his eyes scanning all around us. Shaking his head with a dejected sigh, he said, "The only way out is through the main gate, but with how many men are out there, it'd be suicide."

"What we need..." Jack started, drawing our attention to him. "Is a distraction."

Without warning, Jack's wings sprouted, and he took flight. Zipping toward the fighting, he drew most of the guards toward him, leaving the palace gate free and clear.

As they charged him, Jack threw a blast of frost through the air, fast freezing the first two guards, and as they started to plummet toward the earth, he doubled back, arcing through the air, warhammer raised high. The guards, temporarily stunned by their leaders turning to ice sculptures, hesitated, and that was all Jack needed to press his advantage.

His warhammer lashed out in a brutal overhead swing that shattered the skull of the next guard in line, and as his corpse plummeted like a bloody comet, he whirled, flying into the crowd of men and lashing out with the haft of his weapon. As the blow caught the closest guard under the chin and snapped his head back with a brutal crack, I realized what he was doing. Using them for cover to keep the others from blasting him.

"That brilliant idiot." Raiden shook his head, and I couldn't agree more even as my heart sank to my stomach. At the end of the day, Jack was surrounded, and even though the ice dragon seemed a great warrior, numbers had a way of getting the upper hand given enough time. We just had to make sure they didn't have that much time. As bolts of frost sprang from my suiter's hands, dropping more of the guards, I pressed forward, urging Firestar on.

"Let's not let his sacrifice go to waste." Firestar bounded forward not at all worried about his words. Sacrifice? Jack was just distracting them, that was all. He'd come back. He had to come back.

I told myself this over and over as we made it to the gate. Raiden rushed up the ladder of the gate tower. A moment later a latch clicked loudly, and the gate rose. Not waiting for Raiden to return to the ground, Firestar grabbed hold of my hand and pulled me through the archway and into the city.

With a firm hold on my hand, Firestar wouldn't let me slow down for a second. As he shouldered aside one of the guards outside, he shoved me forward. As the guy hit the ground, Firestar whirled, driving the blade of his kusarigama into the second guard's chest. Blood spurted from the wound, and as the guard collapsed to his knees clutching his gushing chest, Firestar moved to my side.

"We have to hurry," he said, urging me onward. I tried to keep pace with him as best I could, but I kept looking back to search for Raiden or Jack. When we finally made it far enough away from the palace itself, we paused to catch our breaths.

"Do you think…?" I started to ask, but Firestar cut me off.

"Don't think about it. We have to get you out. That's what's important." When I opened my mouth to argue, he grabbed me by the shoulders. "Maya, they are doing this for you. Don't let their sacrifices be in vain."

My eyes pricked with tears and I was on the verge of a meltdown when Raiden landed right in the middle of us. Laughing through my tears, I wrapped my arms around Raiden's waist, holding onto him as if he might disappear at any moment.

"Sorry for the delay, I got stopped on the way down." Raiden patted me on the back and then nodded at Firestar. "Has Jack…?"

"No, not yet," Firestar answered and then for us to keep going.

With Raiden at my back and Firestar at my front, we dodged behind houses and market stalls. It was quieter here, most of the fighting near the palace. In fact, we didn't see a guard until the city limits were in sight.

"It doesn't seem like the fighting has made it this far yet." Firestar pointed out the lack of extra guards on the outer wall. "But I doubt it will stay that way for long."

"I agree." Raiden nodded toward the gate. "Though, getting through the main gate will be a bit harder than the palace. You remember how we were stopped before. At night time, it will be even worse."

"So, how do we get out?" I sighed exasperatedly. I couldn't believe it was this difficult to get out of a city. I didn't remember my father's palace being that hard to leave. Then again, I'd never been there while we were under siege.

"Leave it to me," Raiden said, touching the side of his nose with a wink.

Before I could protest, Raiden started toward the gates as if he had no care in the world. I was getting tired of them leaving me. I had no way of knowing if they were coming back, and if I didn't have them, then what was the point of it all?

Firestar inched us closer to the gates, but we couldn't make out what Raiden was saying to the guards. A few minutes later, he came back out of the shadows and waved us forward. Not looking a gift horse in the mouth, we hurried over to him.

Not meeting their gaze, we followed Raiden through the gates and out of the city. We didn't dare look back or say anything until we were on the hill where we had first seen Raiden's beloved home.

"What did you say to them?" I asked when we could finally breathe.

Raiden smirked and rocked on his heels just exuding self-satisfaction. "My mother might be a vicious, conniving woman, but she doesn't know the first thing about warfare."

I raised a brow not sure what he meant.

"She focused all her effort on closing down the palace and didn't think to bother with the front gate. They didn't even know we were under attack." Raiden chuckled and shook his head. "So, I told them that the raiders had gotten loose and were attacking the palace."

"And?" I coaxed him, not believing the guards could be that dumb.

"And that if my brothers or a guy with long white hair comes this way to let them out immediately because they are supposed to help us against the raiders." Firestar opened his mouth, but Raiden held a finger up to stop him. "But wait, this is the best part."

Firestar and I exchanged an impatient look and then turned our attention back to the boasting lightning dragon.

"I told them if any rumors are going around that don't make sense, not to believe them. The raiders are trying to split the kingdom, and those here on the wall are the last stronghold against them." He smacked his leg and laughed at his own cleverness.

Shaking my head at him, I didn't even bother to explain how not funny it was. Jack and his brothers' safety relied completely on the guards believing his tall tales. Not a pleasant thought.

Turning back to the fighting city, I rubbed the back of my neck. "So, what now? Do we wait to see if your brothers and Jack make it or go on?"

Firestar and Raiden looked at each other a silent message passed between them before Firestar turned back to me. "We need to keep going, put as much distance between us and the palace as possible. Then we can stop and wait for them."

"But what about Jack or your brothers?" I asked, still not convinced. "We can't leave them there. They could get killed."

"Mother won't kill my brothers." He shook his head before continuing. "Even she's not that callous." He paused, mulling over his next words. "I also doubt my mother will want Jack dead now that you've escaped," Raiden said, meeting my eyes. "He's too useful as collateral."

"You mean?" I asked, dread filling my stomach.

"Yes." Raiden nodded solemnly. "Even if they do manage to capture him, he'll be okay, at least until my mother can reach out to bargain with you for his life." He took a deep breath. "The best thing you can do for him is to keep going."

Not happy with the decision but knowing it was for the best, I inclined my head slightly.

We made our way down the other side of the hill, leaving the warring city behind us. Keeping on foot, so not to be seen in the sky, we didn't stop until we were deep into a thick gathering of trees. I focused on putting one foot in front of the other and not what I was leaving behind. If I did, I wouldn't be able to keep going without breaking down.

I had to be strong. That was what Jack would want. What all of them would want. Plus, I didn't want to be a burden to them, and a hysterical woman would definitely be a burden right now.

"Let's stop here," Raiden stated after another hour of travel. "We are a few miles from the city, and my mother doesn't know this place. Fortunately, both Jack and my brothers do," he inclined his head to Firestar who nodded.

"This is where we set up camp before heading after the bandits," Firestar affirmed.

"Exactly, so if they manage to escape, they will come here to check first." Raiden gave me a satisfied look.

"Are you sure?" I asked, surprised.

"Yes." Raiden nodded. "Trust me."

With that, Firestar and Raiden went about making camp while I dug through the bag. I found a bundle of wood but put it aside so we could save it for when there wasn't an abundance of trees. I pushed aside several other items not needed until my hand found a metal flask.

Withdrawing it from the bag, I didn't even hesitate before unscrewing the top and chugging the contents. Hot fire ran down my throat and settled in my belly. The Dragon's Tears worked as fast as I hoped, numbing my emotions enough so I didn't feel like I was falling apart.

I lifted the flask to take another drink, but it was snatched from my hands. Jumping to my feet, I yelled, "Give that back!"

"Do you have any idea what this could do to your child if you were really pregnant?" Jack asked me, holding the flask high above my head as he gave me a chastising glare.

"One drink won't hurt," I argued, standing on my tiptoes trying to get it back before it registered who was talking to me. Eyes wide, I scanned over Jack's form to make sure I wasn't drunk hallucinating, but I wasn't. It was really him. Throwing myself on him, I knocked him back a step, his arms coming down to wrap around me.

"It's all right," Jack soothed, running his hand through my hair. "I'm here. I'm fine."

Suddenly, I shoved him back and smacked his chest. "Don't you ever do anything like that again, you stupid, stupid man!"

"My apologies." Jack chuckled, holding his hands up in defense. "I did not mean for you to worry."

"Well, I did," I snapped back and then threw myself into his embrace once more. "I was scared I'd never see you again."

"Me too, my love. Me too," he murmured into my hair.

My heart swelled. We were safe, and I had all three of my men with me. Nothing could have made me happier at that moment.

Sure, we were surrounded by enemies with even more coming daily, and I didn't know what would be waiting for us in the north. What I did know beyond a shadow of a doubt was that as long as I had Firestar guarding my back and Raiden and Jack at my sides, we'd be able to take on anything that came at us. Together.

THANK YOU FOR READING!

**Curious about what happens to Maya,
Raiden, Jack, and Firestar next?**

Find out in Swallowing Fire!

AUTHOR'S NOTE

Dear reader, if you REALLY want to read the next Starcrossed Dragons novel- I've got a bit of bad news for you. Unfortunately, **Amazon will not tell you when the next comes out.**

You'll probably never know about my next books, and you'll be left wondering what happened to Maya and the gang. That's rather terrible.

There is good news though! There are three ways you can find out when the next book is published:

1) You join our mailing list by clicking here.

2) You can also follow Erin on her Facebook Page. We always announce new books in those places as well as interact with fans.

3) You follow us on Amazon. You can do this by going to the store page (or clicking this link) and clicking on the Follow button that is under the author picture on the left side.

If you follow me, Amazon will send you an email when I publish a book. You'll just have to make sure you check the emails they send.

Doing any of these, or all three for best results, will ensure you find out about my next book when it is published.

If you don't, Amazon will never tell you about my next release. Please take a few seconds to do one of these so that you'll be able to join Maya and the gang on their next adventure.